DEBRA WEBB

Debra Webb wrote her first story at age nine and her first romance at thirteen. It wasn't until she spent three years working for the military behind the Iron Curtain and within the confining political walls of Berlin, Germany, that she realized her true calling. A five-year stint with NASA on the space shuttle program reinforced her love of the endless possibilities within her grasp as a storyteller. A collision course between suspense and romance was set. Debra has been writing romantic suspense and action-packed romantic thrillers since. Visit Debra at www.debrawebb.com.

OUT-FOXXED

DEBRA WEBB

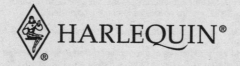

HARLEQUIN®

TORONTO • NEW YORK • LONDON
AMSTERDAM • PARIS • SYDNEY • HAMBURG
STOCKHOLM • ATHENS • TOKYO • MILAN • MADRID
PRAGUE • WARSAW • BUDAPEST • AUCKLAND

ISBN-13: 978-0-373-19892-4
ISBN-10:   0-373-19892-2

OUT-FOXXED

According to Merriam-Webster, the first definition of unique is "being the only one." That definition is followed by others like "being without a like or equal" and "distinctively characteristic." In observing today's trends, I often ask myself: Where is the individuality? Where is the courage to reach deep within oneself and, unashamed, show the world what is discovered? I've recently found that hope is not all lost. This year I met a young man who embodies the term unique...who truly marches to his own beat and forges paths rather than following in anyone else's. This book is dedicated to John Baxley. John, there really is no one else like you.

CHAPTER ONE

THE LULL of the subway train barreling through the tunnel had a hypnotic effect. Despite the press of bodies all around her, Sabrina Fox could almost have fallen asleep right there, standing up and squeezed into the middle of the throng of commuters. Her mind conjured the image of the rain that had forced her onto the subway tonight. Her apartment was only about twelve blocks from work, but no way would she walk in this downpour. As for hailing a cab, forget about it. Managing to snag a cab on a rainy evening at rush hour only happened in the movies.

Real New Yorkers took the train when the weather was uncooperative.

There was nothing colder than a rainy December night in Manhattan. Don't let anybody tell you different. Those miles of asphalt and concrete that absorbed the heat and acted as an oven in the summer had the reverse effect in winter, mercilessly radiating the bitter cold. But with Friday evening commuters packed into the train as if this particular one were their last chance for weekend freedom, staying warm wasn't a problem.

Standing room only. Lots of body heat.

Every stop was a study in warily choreographed footwork. Dozens of people off, dozens on; of course, no one who wanted off was ever the closest person to the door. Stepping on toes was as inevitable as breathing. That was the reason she carried her fashionable stilettos in her briefcase and wore her less-than-attractive sneakers for the trek home every day. She generally walked so it made sense.

She surveyed the people jammed into the subway car along with her. The usual eclectic blend of cultures, financial classes and age ranges. Fashion ranged from the mismatched castoffs of a beggar to the high style purchased on Madison or Fifth Avenue.

Diversity was one of the things Sabrina loved most about New York City, the city that never sleeps. There was no end to things to do. Even after calling the city home for almost ten years, she still stumbled upon a shop she'd never visited before or a cozy café tucked into the least likely place. This was home, more so than the Midwest town where she'd spent the first twenty-two years of her life.

The same afternoon she'd graduated from

college, she'd taken the last plane out of Kansas and headed for the future. Her extensive study of foreign languages—French, German, Russian and Italian—landed her a job at the United Nations as a substitute interpreter. Any time the regular interpreters in her areas of expertise were on sick leave or on vacation, she took up the slack. The rest of the time, she provided translation services for visiting VIPs and their families. Fascinating work. She'd spent three years very happy there until an opportunity she hadn't been able to turn down had come along. An intriguing new world had opened up, one that no one she knew now or in the past could possibly imagine.

A smile slid across her lips. She did love her work.

Beneath the bulky coat she wore, tucked into the pocket of her suit jacket, her cell phone vibrated. There had been a time when the one thing guaranteed by a ride on the subway was the lack of intrusion by one's cell phone. Not always so anymore. With the expansion of service to the platforms and the cutting-edge technology of her special cell phone, there was no escape.

"Perfect."

Keeping her left hand on the overhead grab bar to maintain her balance, with her right she elbowed at least two people in her attempts to unbutton her coat and reach into her jacket pocket.

The train braked hard for the next stop, the flux in momentum causing the crowd to lean forward and then snap back. Despite the shift of bodies as some passengers moved toward the doors and others scooted into their vacated spots, she managed to open the phone and get it to her ear.

"Fox."

"The henhouse is unguarded."

Protocol.

Sabrina immediately took stock of her position. The next stop was approximately three minutes away. "I understand."

The automated voice on the other end of the line gave the address. Protocol was the sophisticated link by which Sabrina received her orders.

She closed the phone and slid it into the pocket of her coat. Hoisting the strap of her briefcase a little higher on her shoulder, she considered the best route for getting off the train quickly. The space between her and the door behind her was crowded with just as many people as the space between her and the door forward of her position. She opted for the door behind her since most of those commuters were younger and only one was accompanied by a child. That group, she estimated, would move a great deal more quickly than the other.

As the train slowed, she executed an about-face. She smiled at the man directly behind her with whom she came face-to-face. Thankfully he smiled back. Inertia had the crowd of commuters who wanted off at this stop weaving as they pushed toward the doors.

Sabrina's heart rate kicked into a faster rhythm with her body's release of adrenaline. Every second wasted could make all the difference.

The doors slid open with a whoosh and the anxious emigration began. The instant her feet hit the platform, she broke into a zigzagging run to get around those who had no place special to be, mothers attempting to push baby strollers while hanging on to their older children and those distracted by conversations.

Sabrina took the steps up to the surface street two at a time. The cold, damp air filled her lungs, replacing the warmer, somewhat more odorous underground air. The rain hadn't let up, still coming down steadily from the dark overcast sky.

Scanning the street for the elusive yellow cab, she hustled down to the nearest corner. She was in a hell of a hurry. Taking the train back to 42nd Street and then changing for one that would land her closer to 52nd would be time-consuming. She didn't have a lot of that precious commodity. She needed a cab. With the continuing rain she might as well be asking God for a miracle.

A cab easing to the curb half a block to her right had her thinking that maybe the movies did get it right from time to time. Or maybe God decided to give her a break.

Sabrina didn't give the other folks coming out of the subway station a chance to give her any competition. She ran the half block, thankful for her practical selection in footwear.

She grabbed for the vehicle's back door before the woman who'd just climbed out could push it closed.

"Hey, lady," the driver shouted. He pointed to the roof of his cab. "I'm off duty."

Dammit.

Not wanting him to take off without her, she slid into the backseat anyway, much to his surprise.

"What the hell you doin'? I told you I'm off duty."

"Get me to 52nd and Madison in under fifteen minutes—" she passed a one-hundred dollar bill to him through the open space in the Plexiglas partition "—and I'll give you another one just like it."

Their gazes met in the rearview mirror, his wary, hers determined. "Besides the fare?" he asked.

A satisfied grin toyed with her lips. "Besides the fare."

He accepted the hundred. "No problem, lady."

Sabrina relaxed in the seat, pulled the safety belt across her and snapped it into place. She didn't question the driver's chosen route. It wasn't the one she would have picked, but then she didn't drive a taxi for a living. He would know the best direction for beating the traffic. At this hour, he'd be lucky to make it in her specified time limit unless he sprouted wings. But then, it was almost Christmas and money could be a serious motivator.

Anticipation had her counting the streets as the driver weaved in and out of traffic in an effort to maintain his dicey speed…39th…42nd. The blare of horns and the occasional near brush with another vehicle kept the ride interesting.

So far, so good.

Most of the street vendors had closed up shop. A hot dog cart on the corner of 45th still had a customer or two seemingly oblivious to the rain. The ambitious gentlemen who generally hawked knockoffs of designer purses, sunglasses and the like had already packed up their wares and headed home. The few who stuck it out offered umbrellas and ponchos for those who hadn't watched the weather forecast the night before.

The crush of pedestrians on the sidewalks reminded her again that there were only a few more shopping days until Christmas. She should pick up something for her niece and nephew. Overnighting the gifts would be her only option for ensuring they arrived on time at this late date.

Maybe she should also pick up gift cards for the members of her team. Letting the holiday slip by unacknowledged by her wouldn't sit well with her relatives or her colleagues. She'd learned that unpleasant lesson last year.

When they hit 49th Street, the driver started to make his way toward Madison. Four blocks from her destination, they hit trouble—a one-way street with the first of two lanes blocked by a large delivery truck and the other clogged with an accident. The drivers of the two vehicles involved in the fender bender stood in the rain yelling at each other.

Just what she needed. At least the rain had let up.

"I'll walk from here." She checked the meter before passing her driver the second hundred as well as the fare. She had to give him credit; with superb driving skills and nerves of steel, he would have made it under the time limit if not for the accident. "Thanks."

He executed one of those half nods in acknowledgement of her appreciation and stuck the money into his shirt pocket. As she got out, he laid down on the horn, joining the unpleasant harmony of the other five or six drivers who were already expressing their displeasure with the delay in traffic.

Sabrina ran the final four blocks.

She slowed as she reached the grand entrance to the Omni Berkshire Hotel, took a breath and squared her shoulders. "Showtime."

The doorman flashed a wide, pleasant smile and opened the door for her entrance. "Good evening, madam, welcome to the Omni Berkshire Hotel."

She thanked him and entered the marble-floored lobby. Chandeliers glittered overhead, and a profusion of flowers provided a welcoming ambience. As she paused at the registration desk, the clerk welcomed her with the same enthusiasm as the doorman.

Sabrina returned the pleasant smile. "I have a reservation. Cynthia Freeman."

A few clicks of the computer keys and he confirmed her reservation. "Yes, here we are."

She passed him the credit card embossed with the name Cynthia Freeman and about ninety seconds later she had a keycard to Room 608.

The elevator car was waiting, another stroke of good luck. She boarded alone and was glad that it didn't stop between the lobby and the floor she'd chosen. Outside Room 608 she slid the keycard through the lock, watched for the green light and went inside.

The room was already abuzz with activity.

"Agent Fox has arrived."

Sabrina winked at Benjamin Trainer as she dropped her briefcase near the door. He was the communications specialist attached to IT&PA, International Temps and Personal Assistants. He could do just about anything with a satellite link. She imagined there were a number of other things he could do quite well, but being coworkers precluded her investigation into the interesting possibility.

"Trainer, you're looking smart this evening." She surveyed his lean athletic frame as she pulled off her gloves and stuffed them into the pockets of her coat before shrugging out of the heavy outerwear.

Evidently the man had a date tonight. In seven years, she couldn't recall seeing him dressed in snug jeans, a pullover sweater that looked exactly like one she'd seen in a Gap ad, and classy loafers. This man never wore anything to work that wasn't a three-piece suit. His dark hair and green eyes were icing on the cake. But then, this was Friday evening. A handsome young guy like him would certainly have plans.

"Depends upon whether or not you wind this up in a timely manner," he quipped, one eyebrow cocked in blatant skepticism.

"No pressure, right?" she teased.

Along with Trainer were two other support personnel on site. A control team would be close by, if not already in place.

"This is your uniform, Agent Fox." Costumer and disguise technician Angie Russell waved her arm to indicate the maid's uniform, shoes and other accessories displayed across the elegant comforter on the king-size bed.

"Thanks, Angie." Sabrina was already stripping off her street clothes.

"Nice shoes." This comment came from operation coordinator Hugo Clay, aka Big Hugh. He stood six-four and weighed about two-fifty. Not the sort of guy one wanted to run into in a dark alley. But Sabrina had figured him out long ago. He was just a big, cuddly teddy bear who could also drop a man in his tracks with nothing but his hands.

Sabrina toed off first one Nike sneaker, then the other. "I wore them just for you, Big Hugh."

"Let's move it, people," Trainer reminded. "Time is of the essence."

Sabrina's suit jacket landed on the floor atop her coat. "Yes, sir, Specialist Trainer. We wouldn't want to keep *her* waiting."

"Fox is prepping now, sir," Trainer said into the mouthpiece of his commo apparatus, ignoring Sabrina's dig. The *sir* he reported to was Director Anderson Marx. Talking to the boss or not, Sabrina didn't miss the way the corners of Trainer's mouth quirked as he spoke. He liked it when she used that official tone with him, even if she were teasing.

As she wiggled out of her skirt, Big Hugh gently placed a listening device into her right ear.

"This will provide you with a constant feed from Trainer and our esteemed Director Marx."

Sabrina kicked aside her skirt and peeled off her black tights. "Give me the details," she said to Hugh as she straightened and freed the buttons of her blouse.

"We have Namir Stavi on the 10th floor," he began.

"Israeli?"

Big Hugh nodded. "He and his wife and two children are here for the Christmas holidays. The Agency picked up on reports that an attempt would be made on Stavi's life while he was visiting our fair city. He and his family are to be executed, and the act is to be blamed on Muslim radicals who hold American visas."

"Nice," she mused. Some jerk was always trying to make someone else look bad on American soil. She could see how the press would be all over that kind of international incident, creating even more tension between the American and the Muslim communities, not to mention the Israelis. Recent events already had Israel a little sensitive where the U.S. was concerned.

"Our polite colleagues thought they had the situation under control," Big Hugh explained, "but somehow the time line got moved up and the assassins hit twenty-four hours early. The agents doing preliminary surveillance couldn't move into place swiftly enough to counter the attack, so here we are."

By "polite colleagues," Big Hugh meant the FBI. If he'd said our arrogant colleagues he would have meant the CIA. His reference to the Agency meant the National Security Agency, the branch of the government to which their organization was loosely attached.

Sabrina grabbed the maid's uniform and plunged her arms into the appropriate holes before tugging the thing over her head.

"Pink must be your favorite color, Fox." This remark came from Trainer. He glanced pointedly at her low-cut pink panties just as she poked her head through the neck of the uniform. "Every time I've seen you undress you're wearing pink panties."

"That constitutes sexual harassment," Angie warned him with a glare as she thrust the uniform's matching cap at Sabrina. From all appearances Angie was a stern woman, stoutly built, just shy of five feet, she had a menacing stare that could wither the staunchest male attitude. She was forty-five if she was a day and mothered the whole lot of them.

Trainer shrugged, his attention shamelessly riveted to Sabrina's hips as she wiggled into the uniform that fit like a glove. "In my opinion, her taking off her clothes in front of me constitutes the same."

Sabrina turned her back to Angie for her to take

care of the zipping and suggested, "Next time, you strip, too, and we'll be even."

Big Hugh's interest visibly heightened. "That sounds fair."

Glee glittered in Trainer's eyes. "Fine. Next time, we'll all just get naked together." He directed an amused look at Angie. "Fair is fair."

"Like hell," Angie muttered.

Sabrina smoothed a pair of nude hose over her legs, then slipped her feet into the white, rubber-soled shoes. "What kind of firepower do we have?"

Big Hugh pinned a button that declared her employee of the month on the crisply starched lapel of her uniform. "That's so we can hear you."

Angie slapped a thigh holster into Hugh's broad hand and stated, "We've got a .32 here." The weapon was dropped into Sabrina's palm next.

Sabrina checked the .32, which was loaded.

"That good?" Hugh asked.

She glanced down at the thigh holster he'd just fastened into place. She sheathed the .32 there and let the skirt of her uniform slither back down over it. "Perfect."

"I'm definitely in the wrong line of work," Trainer commented dryly. "I don't even get to touch the thigh holster, much less strap it on."

Angie cleared her throat, drawing Sabrina's attention back to her, and held up her hand. A lovely ring, gold with a small cluster of diamonds, sat on her palm. "Be careful with this."

Sabrina gingerly picked up the piece of jewelry. "Poison?"

Angie nodded. "Stick your target good." She pointed to what looked like an extra stone on the back of the band. "Depress this at the same time and the poison will be released."

Cautiously sliding the piece of lethal jewelry onto her right ring finger, Sabrina asked, "How long does it take to work?"

"Ten seconds at most. Even a guy the size of Big Hugh will drop like a rock. But don't miss. There's only one dose."

"I assume this means that the protocol for this op is kill first and ask questions later."

Big Hugh nodded. "We know who set up the attack. We know the ultimate goal, leaving no reason to make this any more difficult than necessary. The enemy is totally expendable."

"Do we know how many bogies I'll encounter?"

He shook his head. "Surveillance spotted two, but there could be more we don't know about. Control hasn't been able to get a visual inside the room as of yet. Something about the way the duct work is set up."

It was always good to go into an operation with as much knowledge as possible. But some situations just didn't allow for as much advance information as others.

"I can't risk arming you with anything heavier," Angie interrupted. "They'll most certainly pat you down."

Sabrina nodded. "I understand." She turned her attention to the cleaning cart waiting by the door. "We have a passkey?"

Angie joined Sabrina at the cart. "This is the same cart all the cleaning ladies on staff use. We've rigged it with enough tear gas to put down a herd of elephants, but we don't want to go that route unless absolutely necessary. Protecting the lives of the hostages is top priority, as you know."

Sabrina understood. The moment the bad guys noticed anything off-kilter, the killing would begin. If they killed even one of the hostages before the gas put them down, that was one too many, and the operation would be considered a failure. A SWAT team could go in and neutralize the situation, but that wasn't the goal here. This operation was about rescue, not extermination.

"Room 1012." Big Hugh provided the passkey. "We'll be listening to every word. The cart's rigged for sound, too. If you need us, you know what to do."

"And if I don't need you," Sabrina countered, "I'll let you know." These ops could get tense.

She didn't need a control team moving in if there was any chance she could recover the situation.

"We won't make a move without the code phrase," he assured.

"Let's do this thing, then." Sabrina grasped the handle of the cart and pushed it through the door Trainer held open.

"Good luck, Fox," he murmured as she passed.

She hesitated long enough to whisper back, "I don't need luck, Trainer, I'm Sabrina Fox."

He grinned. "That's right. How could I forget?"

Sabrina pushed the cart into the corridor and the door closed behind her.

"I wish this night was over already," she muttered.

"Sound check is good." Trainer's voice whispered in her ear, compliments of the commo link Big Hugh had tucked there.

"I need a long hot bath and a bottle of wine," she added softly as she parked her cart in front of the elevators and pressed the call button.

A sound of deep, guttural agreement echoed in her ear.

She had to smile. Maybe she'd give Trainer a little tit for tat given that he'd made that smart-ass remark about her panties. She did prefer pink lingerie, that was true. She owned pink panties in every imaginable style. French cut, lacy thong, extreme low-rise.

The elevator doors slid open and she pushed the

cart inside and selected the tenth floor. Since she was alone in the car, she leaned against the wall and sighed dramatically.

"Lots and lots of frothy bubbles. Neck-deep hot water. Oh yeah, that's exactly what I'm going to do when I get home." She closed her eyes and made one of those throaty, wistful sounds that made her think of hot, sweaty sex. "I'll probably start taking my clothes off before I even get through the door to my apartment. Light every candle in the place and take the bottle of wine and two stemmed glasses to the tub with me."

"Is that an invitation, Agent Fox? You did say two glasses."

Director Anderson Marx.

Her gaze snapped open, her face flushed with embarrassment. "Negative, sir, I was…just getting into character with a relaxation technique."

Damn, she'd forgotten Marx was tied in already. Damn Trainer. He should have said something.

She could imagine him, with his mike muted, laughing his ass off.

"Standing by," Big Hugh said, reminding her that he was there as well.

"Ten-four, Big Hugh." She didn't worry about the big guy; she wasn't his type.

The car glided to a stop with a soft ding. She pushed the cart into the alcove outside the bank of elevators. A floor-to-ceiling window was on the right, the corridor running parallel to the front of the building on the left. She took the left and headed for Room 1012.

A few steps later, she arrived at the door. She inhaled a deep, fortifying breath, then let it out slowly. She touched her uniform where the holstered weapon lay snugly against her inner thigh, then knocked loudly on the door. "Housekeeping," she announced.

The room was quiet beyond the door.

Anticipation released another round of adrenaline that ignited a fire in her veins.

She knocked again. "Housekeeping!"

After waiting the perfunctory ten seconds, she slid her passkey through the reader and watched for the green light. Braced for whatever she might find, she pushed down on the lever and backed into the door, ushering it inward as she went.

With her back fully to the room, she pulled her cart through the door. Her pulse edged into that alert zone that reminded her that she'd just turned her back on the enemy. But she needed whoever was in the room to believe she expected to find it empty.

When her cart cleared the open doorway, the door closed with a heavy thud.

"Don't move."

The undeniable feel of a muzzle pressed against the back of her skull.

She caught her breath, adopted an expression of terror, making her eyes go wide and leaving her lips slightly parted.

A hand moved over her torso. She tensed, as much from the need to ensure whoever it was didn't find the weapon fastened against her inner left thigh as from the need to appear frightened.

She twisted slightly away from his touch. "What're you doing?" She was proud of the fear infused in her voice, as well as a second harsh intake of breath that sounded completely credible. "What's going on here?"

Harsh fingers curled around her arm and jerked her around to face the owner of the gun that had left an impression on her scalp. "Shut up," he growled.

She made a small shrieking sound, just loud enough to be convincing without alarming him. Things could go downhill fast if he or one of his friends grew suspicious of her and panicked.

"You have very bad timing, lady." He leered at her, his gaze raking down to her breasts. "You should have skipped this room."

Making her body tremble wasn't difficult considering the guy jammed the silenced muzzle of a Glock 9mm under her chin. Not exactly comfortable—and she didn't trust him not to accidentally fire off a round. Glocks weren't designed for amateurs or idiots. He looked exactly like the latter, a little too excited and gung ho. Considering the uniform she wore, she doubted her breasts had caused the effect.

"I'm sorry," she whimpered. "Please...please... don't hurt me."

He laughed, nice and loud as goons would do. "Please, please don't hurt me," he mimicked in a high-pitched, squeaky voice.

"What do we do with her?"

The new male voice came from behind the goon currently manhandling her.

Well, now she knew for sure there were at least two of them.

The goon with the 9mm still rammed against her glanced menacingly over his shoulder. "What the hell are you doing? Get back in there!"

Sabrina knew this room was a two-bedroom suite. Though she couldn't see anything beyond the large man blocking her view, obviously some or all of the family were being held in one of the bedrooms.

When the goon's attention turned back to her, she dropped back into character. "Please," she pleaded, "I'm just a housekeeper." She shook her head frantically. "I don't—"

"Shut up!" He backhanded her.

She saw at least one star on the heels of the pain that shattered in her jaw. She didn't have to taste the blood to know he'd busted her lip. Nothing major, just a tiny crack.

Marshalling the requisite tears, she dove deeper into the part of terrified hostage.

Her new friend shoved her to the floor next to her cart. "Don't move," he snarled, "while I decide what to do with you."

Shaking for the benefit of those watching, Sabrina huddled against the cool stainless steel of the cart and covertly took a look around the room.

Two men lay on the floor near the massive wall of windows that, behind the drawn drapes, over-looked Manhattan. Both men were bound and gagged, and either dead or unconscious.

The unmistakable sound of a hard fist connect-ing with soft flesh tugged her attention to her extreme right.

An older man was secured to a chair. His face bore the signs of a severe beating, yet he somehow managed to look distinguished in his distress. As she watched, he groaned and attempted to turn away from the next blow coming his way.

Mr. Stavi.

Well, at least he was still alive.

The guy beating him made Goon Number Three. The taller guy standing back watching the torture was Number Four.

Four to one.

Not the worst odds she'd ever encountered.

But not the best, either.

Since the wife and children were not in this

room, her initial assessment had likely been correct. The family, dead or alive, was being held in one of the bedrooms. Since Goon Number One had ordered Goon Number Two back to his post, she would work under the assumption that he still had live hostages to oversee.

The sound of a round being chambered hauled her attention once more to the man hovering over her. She stared into the ominous black barrel of the 9mm, then at the bully beyond it.

"I've made up my mind," he declared.

CHAPTER TWO

"GET UP."

In her earpiece, Big Hugh reminded her that all she had to do was say the word and a team would move in and do the takedown.

"I'll do anything you say," she offered, sending a pleading look at the man with the gun and a definite message to Big Hugh that the team should stand down for now. She refused to allow the new wave of fight or flight that surged to divert her focus. She had to be ready for any scenario. "Just don't hurt me."

"Get up," her captor roared.

Sabrina scrambled to her feet, mindful of the thigh holster she didn't want making an appearance. Sheer determination kept her heart rate far calmer than it should have been, ensuring a clear head. She'd learned long ago the secrets to remaining cool and collected in the face of death. The enemy could only kill her once and only if she allowed herself to screw up. No matter the situation, some amount of control always belonged to her, no one could take that away.

The fear and panic she permitted on the surface were for the enemy's benefit. She needed these men to continue to believe that she was just a hotel maid, an innocent civilian who had no clue what was going on here. As long as they felt in control, their actions would be more predictable.

"Take her into the bedroom with the others," Goon Number One, the man who appeared to be in charge, told his minion. The boss was older than the others. Streaks of gray had invaded the raven-colored hair along his temples. His grim face told her he'd had more than his share of experience in this sort of activity. Despite his age, he looked lean and fit physically. What was more, his heritage was impossible to calculate. He didn't look Middle Eastern and he certainly didn't sound so.

Goon Number Four, the man she decided to call Tall Guy since he was well over six feet, grabbed her by the arm and hauled her toward the French doors that separated what was likely the master suite from the parlor. Inside the elegant spacious bedroom, a woman and two children cowered in the farthest corner from the door.

The wife and kids of the man currently being tortured.

Also in the room was Goon Number Two, the

one she'd heard ordered back to his post before getting a visual on him. His age was easy to guess, maybe twenty-two or twenty-three. His inexperience was even easier to see. He handled his weapon as if he weren't sure how to hold it or what to do with it next. His eyes were wide with his attempts at taking in everything at once.

Goon Number Two was scared.

Unfortunately, that wasn't necessarily a good thing. His inexperience could cause any number of mistakes. Not to mention that his presence reconfirmed the odds against her—four to one.

But hey, what good was a challenge without interesting odds?

The French doors abruptly shut behind her, sending her tension to a new level. With the doors closed, it would be difficult to hear what was going on in the other room. She would simply have to depend upon Big Hugh to keep her informed for now since he was monitoring that room via the rigged cart.

"Over there," Goon Number Two commanded, directing her to join the other hostages.

Keeping up the necessary facade of fear, she edged past him and moved hesitantly toward the woman and children.

As she passed the en suite bath, she noticed three men, well dressed and obviously dead; they didn't move and were unrestrained, piled on the floor in front of the elegant marble vanity. The three dead guys most likely were—had been—Stavi's security detail. What a shame. Even a family's own personal security couldn't keep them safe in the finest of hotels.

Sabrina scrutinized the woman and her children. She saw no signs of mistreatment. That was good. She hoped like hell she could make sure it stayed that way. "It's going to be okay," she whispered, hoping to reassure the woman with the words and her determined expression.

"No talking!"

Sabrina sent Goon Number Two a scornful glare but he was too busy watching his friends through the French doors to notice. She got the distinct impression he didn't like being left on babysitting duty. He wanted in on the important stuff like the torture. He wanted to be in the middle of the part that really mattered, killing an Israeli VIP.

Too bad for him.

The little girl, who was six or seven years old, Sabrina guessed, started to sob. Her mother tried to reassure her to no avail.

"Shut that kid up," Goon Number Two growled, "or I'll shut her up for you."

Well, wasn't he the tough guy. Terrifying women and children surely made him the man of the hour. *Not*.

Sabrina analyzed the dialect. Not Middle Eastern or European, she was reasonably sure. Even those who'd lived in this country for many years had a difficult time dumping the accents they'd learned growing up. There was training for that purpose, but these people sounded like heartland citizens. Midwestern U.S., maybe.

Were these guys homegrown terrorists? Somehow the idea made her all the more furious, sick to her stomach.

The woman picked up her little girl and held her close. But that left the little boy, who looked to be only four or five, standing alone and clinging to his mother's leg. He would probably start crying, too, as soon as he figured out his mother would have trouble picking both him and his sister up at the same time. Poor kids. And at Christmas at that. Sabrina wanted to hurt these guys just for that.

But antagonizing these goons would not be helpful, though she already understood that their mission included killing not only Stavi but his wife and children, as well. Delaying that move as long as possible was essential. To do that, she had to play submissive and cooperative. Sabrina wanted the trouble to go down later rather than sooner. She needed time to prepare a strategy that included saving all the hostages.

"I have to go to the bathroom."

The plan was hasty and lacked originality, came pretty much out of nowhere, but at least it was a step.

Goon Number Two glared at her. "Shut up," he hissed from between clenched teeth.

Not to be thwarted so easily, she did this little bounce from the knees, the universal gotta-go gesture. "Please, I have to go."

Another of those icy glares. "So go, just don't step on the bodies." He smirked and nodded toward the bathroom where the three men lay in a pile. "And leave the door open where I can see you."

Making her way across the room, Sabrina stayed close to the wall, as far from Goon Number Two as possible. Once in the bathroom, she stepped over the dead men and scooted in next to the toilet. Knowing that her guard was likely watching, she hunkered down over the toilet which was, thankfully, shielded to some degree by the wide vanity and added plenty of realism to her ploy. While she pretended to relieve herself, she sized up the three men on the floor. Whatever weapons they'd been carrying appeared to have been taken.

She righted her clothes, tore off a piece of toilet paper and used it to protect the tips of her fingers as she flushed the toilet. She wouldn't be leaving any prints lying around. The guard glanced in her direction but immediately returned his attention to the goings-on in the parlor. While the sound of rushing water provided some amount of cover, she whispered, "Four. Possibly American-born. Hostages still viable."

"Roger that, Fox," came Trainer's voice in her earpiece. "We're running voice analysis right now."

There was always the chance that a terrorist would be in one or more data systems, including voice recordings, but the chances of a voice match were more unlikely than not.

Careful not to make any sudden moves, Sabrina eased back into the bedroom to join the other woman and her children in the corner between the king-size bed and the wall of windows. As in the parlor, the curtains were drawn for privacy, blocking out the magnificent view of the city she loved.

Goon Number Two opened one side of the French door and said something to his cohorts in what sounded like butchered Arabic. Since Sabrina was not that familiar with the language, she could only guess at some of the phrases. Hugh would keep her informed. She seized the opportunity and whispered to the woman, "I'm here to help you."

The woman's breath caught and her watery gaze locked with Sabrina's. Her lips parted as if she might say something but, thankfully, she held back whatever had been on the tip of her tongue. Relief rushed into her wide dark eyes.

Sabrina's options were pretty much limited at the moment. If she gave the word for the tear gas to be released, Stavi would likely end up dead. Maybe even the woman and children. And, of course, her.

Best thing to do was ride it out a few minutes more.

The exchange continued in the language she didn't understand. The fact that they had stopped speaking in English was a bad sign.

"Fox, can you get a little closer to the man speaking? There appears to be a malfunction in the listening device we planted on the cart," Big Hugh said in her ear piece.

She coughed, which meant not likely.

Goon Number Two glanced at her.

"The man nearest you has asked how the hell they plan to get out of there and why it's taking so long. He's nervous, it seems."

Nervous was definitely a good assessment. Goon Number Two was antsy as hell, partially motivated by his feelings of being left out.

"We're going to send Angie to the door with towels in an effort to get you back into the parlor."

Sabrina cleared her throat, giving the "affirmative" signal.

Since Goon Number Two was still chatting

with his friends, Sabrina decided to make some preparations for the children. She eased closer to the woman, keeping an eye on their guard while she whispered as softly as she could and still be heard, "Have the children sit down on the floor close to the bed. Tell them to crawl under the bed if anything happens."

The woman nodded. She murmured in her daughter's ear, since she still held the child in her arms. The mother settled the girl onto her feet and she immediately did as Sabrina had suggested. The little girl tugged her brother down to the floor next to the bed alongside her. Obviously knowing her children would not stay in that position unless she was as close as possible, the mother scooted in as near as she could.

The discussion between the four men appeared to be turning less and less friendly. Though Sabrina didn't understand the words, she couldn't have missed the tension in the exchange.

"Looks like we have a whole new ballgame here, Fox."

Sabrina focused on Big Hugh's voice while maintaining a visual on Goon Number Two.

"Our man Stavi apparently has some information these guys want. The man in the room with you mentioned that if he didn't talk soon, they would have to move without the information or risk being captured."

That meant that the stakes had just been upped. If Stavi had intelligence these men needed, then allowing any one of them to leave this hotel room would be a mistake with ramifications more far-reaching than they'd first thought.

"Marx wants one alive if possible."

Great. How the hell was she supposed to keep one goon alive?

She cleared her throat just loudly enough for Big Hugh to hear. She had her orders, no point arguing. All she could do was her best. Protecting the lives of the hostages was priority one as far as she was concerned.

The knock on the door to the room silenced the men.

"Housekeeping!"

The boss, looking annoyed and harried, appeared at the French doors and pointed at Sabrina. "You! Come!" he demanded harshly, his voice kept low to ensure that whoever was at the door didn't hear him.

Sabrina, maintaining her scared-to-death demeanor, hurried over to the doors. "That's my coworker with the extra towels I ordered for this room." She moistened her shaking lips and drew in a ragged breath. "If I don't go to the door, she'll just assume I'm finished and come on in anyway."

Fury streaked across the man's face. "Get rid of her or she dies."

Sabrina nodded frantically.

The boss ushered her to the door. He stepped back so that the opening door would block him from view. He indicated the gun in his hand just in case Sabrina had forgotten.

She reached for the lever, took a moment to visually brace herself for her attentive audience's benefit, then pulled the door open.

"Oh! Mary, you're still in here." Angie stood in the doorway, her short, stocky frame filling out a maid's uniform, her arms loaded down with fluffy white towels.

"Yeah," Sabrina said, "the bathroom's a mess. Those kids wrecked the place. It's taking longer than I expected."

"I've got your towels."

When she took a step, Sabrina moved to meet her, from all appearances blocking her path. "That's okay, I'll take them."

Angie passed her the towels. "Well, if you've got it under control, I'll move on. Natalie's got problems in ten and fourteen, as well."

"Thanks, Ang."

When she walked away Sabrina closed the door. So, the control team was in position in the rooms on either side of them. Angie purposely didn't specify the floor to throw off the men listening.

The control team would prepare to launch

devices into the room for auditory as well as visual monitoring. If they made a single wrong move or sound, the guys in here could go ballistic. But it was a necessary step at this point. Attempting to position any sort of device before an agent was in place would have risked the hostages' lives. With Sabrina inside to do what she could to protect the hostages, the next step had to be taken.

The tall guy grabbed the towels and shuffled through the stack. Sabrina used the opportunity to check on Stavi's condition. He looked a little the worse for wear while Goon Number Three, the man who'd been beating him, looked revved for the next round. At this rate Stavi would be dead very soon.

"Please," Sabrina said to the boss. "I don't have anything to do with this. Just let me go. I'll leave. I won't say a word to anyone."

The boss nodded toward the master suite and the tall guy hustled her off in that direction. The thuds and groans of new torture resumed behind her.

The woman, looking wide-eyed and wringing her hands, stood exactly where Sabrina had left her.

The tall guy shoved her toward the bed and then made some remark to Goon Number Two about her having a great ass. This he did in English, so she understood he wanted her to know he'd made the statement.

As soon as Sabrina was next to the woman, she whispered, "My husband?" Her face reflected her anxiety about his fate.

Sabrina arranged her expression into a mask of optimism. "He's okay so far."

The intense discussion between the men recommenced. Sabrina was pretty sure this swiftly deteriorating situation wouldn't last much longer. Stavi would be dead and then they would all die.

"Oh, hell."

Sabrina stiffened. Whatever had just gone down had Big Hugh worried.

"Fox, they've just asked your guard to bring in one of the children. We're standing by for your instruction."

A new kind of tension roiled through Sabrina.

"We'll be okay," she said to the woman, but her real agenda was to let the team know that no movement on their part was necessary, she had the situation under control for now.

Goon Number Two stalked over to where Sabrina, the woman and her children cowered in fear.

"What're you doing?" Sabrina asked, her voice infused with terror.

"The boy," the man demanded. "Give me the boy."

The mother howled in agony. "No, no, no, not my son. Not my son!"

The man slapped her hard. "The boy," he commanded.

"Wait." Sabrina reached toward the man.

He reared back to slap her. She lunged at him, her right hand fisted, the pad of her thumb set against that extra stone on the back of the ring she wore. She rammed her fist, ring first, into his throat.

The back of his hand connected with her cheekbone sending pain radiating up the side of her head. Then he froze. He stared at her for a moment as if he didn't understand what had just happened. When he started to reach for his neck, his eyes rolled back in his head and he collapsed to the floor.

The woman and children started to wail and sob, Sabrina joining the cacophony.

The tall guy barged into the room. "What the hell is going on in here?" He spotted his pal, then aimed a suspicious glare at the women. "Shut up!" He leveled his weapon on Sabrina. "Move against the wall."

Sabrina flattened against the wall next to the window behind her. She reached for the woman and ushered her back as well. A child clung to either side of her. All were sobbing hysterically.

"What happened?" the tall guy demanded, his question directed at Sabrina.

"I don't know." She forced her voice to quiver. "He came over here to get the boy and he just stopped, looked kind of strange and then crumpled to the floor."

That she hadn't reached for the downed man's weapon would lend credence to her innocent by-stander status.

Keeping an eye on her, the tall guy squatted down just far enough to touch his fallen comrade's neck. He felt for a pulse, a frown overtaking his expression.

Speaking in that broken foreign tongue again, he called out to his pals in the other room.

The torturer in the other room stormed in next. "What is taking so long? I need the boy." He drew up short when he saw Goon Number Two on the floor.

Sabrina held on to one of the woman's arms and made small sounds of terror; the woman did the same. The children continued to whimper and sob, amping up the frustration level of the enemy.

Sabrina figured that this was as good as it was going to get. Only one, the boss, was left in the room with Stavi.

She pulled downward on the other woman's arm. Their gazes locked. Sabrina nodded to the floor. The woman moved her head up and down in acknowledgement.

Her right hand easing down to the hem of her uniform, Sabrina watched the two men prepare to drag their friend away, probably to join the dead security detail in the en suite bath.

As soon as each man had crouched down and hooked an arm under the dead guy's, she snatched her .32 out of its holster. Two rounds, one in the temple for the tall guy, one smack in the middle of the forehead for the torturer who turned to look up at her in surprise.

She was halfway across the room when the boss suddenly loomed in the open doorway, his weapon leveled on her. Two more shots, this time straight through the heart. She hit the floor and rolled just in time to avoid the round he managed to squeeze off before he dropped. Unlike the jarring blasts from her .32, a swift hiss and pop were the only sounds his silenced weapon made.

Back on her feet, she holstered her weapon and rushed to the corner where the woman and children huddled together near the floor.

"Everything's all right," Sabrina assured. "Come on, let's check on your husband."

Thank God the woman and children hadn't been in the way of the single shot the bastard had managed. One of the lavish pillows on the bed hadn't been so lucky.

The husband was already shrieking and making all kinds of noise. He kept calling a name—his wife's, Sabrina presumed.

While the woman and children crowded around

the injured man, Sabrina checked the two other hostages bound and still unconscious on the floor to ensure they were still breathing. Both were alive—drugged, she presumed.

Time for her to get out of here.

Other guests would no doubt have called the front desk by now to report the sound of gunshots.

Sabrina propped the door open and prepared to wheel her cart out of the room.

"Please wait."

Sabrina hesitated, then turned to the woman who'd called out to her.

She hurried to where Sabrina stood poised to get the hell out of there. "Thank you." The tears rolling down her cheeks and the quiver of her lips told Sabrina that she wanted to say much more but wasn't sure how.

Sabrina smiled. "You'll be fine now."

She had to get out of there.

Pushing the cart with all her might, she hurried to the elevators and stabbed the call button. "Come on, come on," she muttered.

The control team in the rooms on either side of 1012 would stay put until hotel security had arrived and called the local authorities. Once the Federal Bureau of Investigation was on site to take charge, the control team would withdraw.

No one would ever know that IT&PA had ever been there.

That was the way it worked.

Anticipation seared through her as she trekked the slow movement of the damned elevator on the digital readout above the closed doors. If security caught her up here, they would want to question her. She couldn't let that happen. Abandoning the cart wasn't doable since it was rigged. She had no choice but to ride this out.

One of the two elevators stopped on her floor and she held her breath as she waited for the doors to slide open and reveal the occupants, if any, of the car.

Empty.

Her arms weak with relief, she shoved the cart into the empty elevator and selected floor six. No sooner had the doors started to close when a ding announced the arrival of the second elevator.

Close. Too close.

Even as her car started to descend, she heard running steps pounding in the corridor beyond the elevator alcove she'd just vacated.

Hotel security had arrived.

Director Marx wouldn't be happy that she'd had to take out all four of the perpetrators, but there hadn't been any other option.

Those men would have killed her and the hostages had she not used deadly force. Wounding one of them in hopes of interrogating him later simply hadn't been feasible.

Outside 608, she had just reached for her passkey when the door opened.

"He's not happy," Trainer said.

Angie had already grabbed the other end of the cart and was helping Sabrina guide it into the room.

"It was my call to make," Sabrina countered, not the least bit intimidated or sorry she'd chosen the course of action she had. Stavi was alive. He surely knew what those men wanted with him. All the Bureau had to do was convince him to share the information. As far as Sabrina was concerned, that was their problem.

She'd done her job. All four hostages were rescued.

Angie, still sporting a maid's uniform, rushed over to help Sabrina disrobe.

Trainer turned his back and focused on unrigging the cart. Big Hugh jumped into the fray and helped get the job done.

When all the equipment and disguises were packed in typical wheeled, upright luggage, each member of the recovery team left with at least one bag in tow.

All but Sabrina, who carried only her briefcase as she took the elevator down to the lobby and stopped by the front desk. "I'm leaving very early in the morning," she told the clerk. "Can you clear me without my having to bother checking out?"

"Certainly, Miss Freeman. We'll slip the final bill under your door by 3 a.m."

"Excellent."

Sabrina strode out of the hotel, her sneakers silent on the shiny marble floor. The same doorman who'd greeted her what felt like a lifetime ago, bid her a good evening. She gave him a smile of thanks and hurried off into the gloomy night.

The rain was gone, leaving the city she loved with a crisp bite in the air and smelling pretty damned clean for a place that teemed with no less than eight million people.

Once in a while, a taxi cruising for a fare rolled by on the street, the tires cutting through the water puddled there.

She didn't bother hailing one. She would walk, at least for a while, to give herself time to unwind and to let the cold air remind her that she was still alive. That was the great part about her work. She came so close to death at times…close enough to appreciate living one more day. Not everyone understood how that felt. It was the most satisfying feeling she'd ever known. Maybe that made her a freak, if so, that was okay.

The scene back at the hotel would be one of chaos until the feds arrived to take control of the situation. The Stavi family would only know that a maid had saved their lives.

Sabrina hadn't touched anything in the room so there wouldn't be any prints left behind, not that it mattered. She didn't exist in any of the traditional spy world databases. IT&PA wasn't known in any capacity whatsoever by its sibling agencies.

All involved in the rescue would do exactly as Sabrina was doing now—disappear in the night…until next time.

CHAPTER THREE

THE HOT WATER slowly but surely warmed the winter chill that had seeped deep into her bones, relaxing her tense muscles. Sabrina had ended up walking the entire twenty blocks home.

Without the rain, it hadn't been so bad. She'd needed the time to clear her head. To rid her lungs of the smell of death.

She studied her arms and the new bruises there. So far her cheek hadn't swollen. There would be some discoloration from the slaps she'd taken but, if her luck held out, no noticeable swelling. Bruises could be covered, swelling could not. She was damned lucky things hadn't been a hell of a lot worse.

Just part of the job. Pain and death were a constant in her line of work. She'd gotten used to it a long time ago.

At least that was what she told herself. Occasionally she'd let the kill-or-be-killed reality get to her, but then she would remind herself that what she had done had saved a man and his family. That was what really counted.

The only part that counted to Sabrina.

The first time she'd killed a man, Marx had walked her through the aftereffects.

Sabrina closed her eyes and tried to block the memory but it came anyway. The assignment had been in Ireland. The target had been an American traitor leading a terrorist cell who had recently obtained a military-grade nerve gas. Sabrina had gotten in, made the strike and gotten out in twenty-four hours. Eliminating that target had allowed local authorities to seize the highly lethal nerve gas before it could be used to take innocent lives.

She'd been fine until she returned home.

The reality of what she'd done had hit her then. Marx had known it would. He'd been waiting for her at her apartment door.

During the verbal exchange about how she was fine, she'd fallen apart. He'd talked her through the turmoil, helped her to see the greater good she had accomplished. His wise and calm reasoning had done the trick.

Sabrina blinked away the memory. Funny thing, she realized just then—her father had done that for her dozens of times growing up. He would talk her through a trying time. She supposed, in a way, Marx had stepped into his shoes.

"Way too deep, Sabrina," she mumbled. She needed to relax and put work behind her.

She'd certainly created the right atmosphere for it. The candles flickered and glowed, filling the room with a cozy ambience. The scented ones oozed their subtle fragrance into the air, adding to the pleasant mood. She'd left the overhead lights off, allowing only the illumination of the dozens of candles. Just like she'd told Trainer she wanted to do.

She smiled and wondered if he'd managed to make his date. Big Hugh was likely out with his significant other, enjoying a quiet dinner for two at some ritzy restaurant off the beaten path. Angie would be at home with her husband of twenty years and their three kids, maybe watching a movie with a tub of buttered popcorn.

Sabrina couldn't fathom how Angie managed it. Her husband couldn't know about her work. He thought her employer was an international temps and personal assistants agency. An agency that provided support personnel for visiting dignitaries from other nations or provided support personnel for American businessmen traveling to foreign countries whose companies had no ongoing reason to keep one or more linguists on staff. And that was exactly what IT&PA did in addition to covert government operations.

It was the perfect cover. Movement in and out of a country was never seen as suspicious, and many times their targets were the ones doing the hiring. Now that was burrowing in deep. That was the ultimate cover, one the enemy didn't suspect for a moment. The usual government agencies couldn't hope to accomplish that depth of infiltration.

Not everyone employed at IT&PA were secret agents. Some were "exempt" employees, meaning they were exactly what they appeared to be— clerical personnel with additional skills such as multilingual abilities as well as in-depth knowledge of foreign countries. Oftentimes a job consisted of nothing more than serving as an official guide on a visit to another country. Anything a businessman or woman, American or otherwise, could need in the way of temporary assistance would be found at IT&PA.

The agency had been the brainchild of Anderson Marx, the director. Only the president himself, and the directors of the CIA, FBI and NSA were aware of IT&PA's presence in the spy world. IT&PA was neither bound by borders nor inhibited by the usual rules. Sabrina and her colleagues could be assigned anywhere in the world at any time, and only in the situations where the usual means would not work or had failed. The latter was the reason the standard rules didn't apply. IT&PA was only called in once there were no other alternatives.

Today's mission could have been so much worse. She'd been lucky. The four men who'd taken the Stavi family hostage could have killed them all before she'd arrived. The fact that they hadn't suggested two possibilities—the intelligence they'd hoped to obtain had been extremely valuable, or the men simply were inept.

Telling herself it wasn't her problem now, she ducked her head under the water and banished all thoughts of the day's mission. The big brown eyes of those children and their mother elbowed their way into her thoughts, interrupting her desperately needed relaxation. She'd saved them. Why the lingering feelings of uncertainty?

Because it could have so easily gone the other way.

She went through this every time children were involved in a mission. After seven years, one would think she would get over the after-the-fact apprehension. But she didn't.

If she mentioned the feelings to her team, Angie would insist that it was nothing more than her biological clock screaming at her since those feelings were unfailingly related to missions involving children. Sabrina was thirty-two, after all, Angie would say.

Sabrina didn't know how to tell Angie this, but she didn't have a biological clock. It had given up hope and gone out of business years ago. She had no desire for those kinds of strings. No permanent attachments allowed her to accept any and all assignments without hesitation.

The trickle of denial that filtered through her ticked her off. She wasn't about to let the past intrude on her present.

Not ever again.

Sabrina climbed out of the tub. Frothy bubbles slid down her skin and accumulated on the floor as she stepped onto the cool tile. She should eat. The wine and the bath had been very nice and very necessary, but she needed food. She'd learned from experience in the past couple of years that food could be an extremely reliable way to distract herself from things she didn't want to think about. Her intense workouts allowed for that occasional indulgence.

Grabbing a couple of big fluffy towels, she wrapped her hair in one, turban-style, and swabbed her body with the other. As she did, she considered what frozen entrées she had in the fridge. There might be the makings of a salad if the expiration dates hadn't passed too many days ago. She spent so many late nights at work she didn't stock the refrigerator regularly and as soon as she did, she ended up throwing half of the food out a week or two later after returning from an unexpected mission.

The doorbell rang as she shuffled out of her room.

A frown tugged at her brow. It was almost nine and she just wanted to vegetate for the rest of the evening. Why the heck would anyone be at her door now?

Then she remembered.

She stalled in the middle of her living room. No way was she going to answer that door.

This was the one downside to being single. Well-meaning friends. If her single friends were involved in ongoing relationships, they wanted everyone else to be as well. Not one, especially the one likely outside the door just now, could understand how Sabrina could be happy without a steady guy in her life. She couldn't tell them that a steady relationship created unnecessary questions.

A new round of pounding on the door rattled the hinges. "Sabrina! I know you're in there."

Damn. This was a new low even for Veronica.

Veronica Call and Sabrina had started out at the UN together as substitute interpreters. They'd stayed friends after Sabrina was recruited by IT&PA.

"I'll just keep banging until you open up!" Veronica warned. "Or your neighbors call the cops."

Knowing she wasn't kidding, Sabrina released both dead bolts, then wrenched the door open. "I was in the tub." Not exactly a lie.

Veronica, hands pushed beneath a heavy fur coat and stationed on red silk clad hips, surveyed her skeptically. "You knew I was coming," she accused. "We planned this evening days ago."

"I forgot, okay?" Sabrina stepped back, allowing her furious friend to enter.

Once inside the door, Veronica pointed to Sabrina's bedroom. "Go get dressed. You're going out."

For about five seconds, Sabrina considered telling her to forget it but then decided against it. Veronica was one pushy broad. If she didn't get her way, she'd just stand here all night and argue her case. The woman must have been a trial lawyer in another life.

"Where are we going?" Sabrina asked, padding to her bedroom and leaving the door open so they could still talk.

"Blue Note. Wesley's meeting me there."

Wesley. Oh, yes. Sabrina remembered him. Tall, handsome, gorgeous golden eyes, sleek ebony skin.

"What I don't understand," she said loudly enough for her friend to hear, "is why you want me there. Isn't Wesley enough for you?" Sabrina grinned as she rummaged for something to wear.

"Wesley has a friend."

She should have seen that one coming. Dread pooled in Sabrina's gut, and she glanced at the other woman who now leaned in the doorway, her arms crossed defiantly over her chest.

"That's what I was afraid of."

"Come on, Sabrina. David is nice. Really nice."

Sabrina removed one of her favorite little black dresses from its padded hanger. "Nice?" She tossed her friend a skeptical look. She hated being set up.

"Nice and handsome and sexy as hell," Veronica fired back, her temper flaring to match her hot red dress. "I know you'll like him. You just have to give him a chance."

Sabrina smoothed the tight sheath over her hips. "And you've met this David?"

"Well, no, but Wesley told me all about him."

"Wesley told you he's sexy?" Sabrina countered. "Now I'm worried about Wesley."

"You're impossible."

Sabrina stepped into a pair of black stilettos and uncoiled the towel from her hair. "Gotta blow dry."

Fifteen minutes later, dried, styled, and accessorized, Sabrina slipped into her coat and announced, "I'm ready."

"'Bout time." Veronica assessed her from head to toe and back. "You look fabulous. David should be very pleased."

"My greatest aspiration," Sabrina said wistfully as they exited her apartment. "To please a stranger."

THE PREMIER JAZZ CLUB on 3rd and 131st was packed. As a close cousin of the owner, Wesley had reserved the best table in the house. The exciting, spirited atmosphere immediately lifted Sabrina's mood. Even if David hadn't shown. Or maybe she was simply enjoying Veronica's discomfort over the fact that her scheming had failed so miserably. There was nothing more humiliating than masterminding a blind date only to have one half of the couple fail to show.

"I'm sure he'll be here," Wesley said again.

Sabrina wasn't keeping an exact count, but she was pretty sure he'd made this same comment at least seven or eight times.

"Should we go ahead and order?" Veronica asked looking immensely uncomfortable.

Served her right. Maybe this would teach her a lesson.

Sabrina tried not to get too much glee from the circumstances but she just couldn't help herself.

"Yes, let's order." Wesley looked even more appalled than his date.

The waiter arrived as if he'd sensed the shift of intentions at the table. He made his recommendations and then efficiently accepted their orders.

"You know," Sabrina felt compelled to say considering the downtrodden expression worn by her good friends, "this really is okay."

Wesley's expression suddenly brightened. "There he is."

Sabrina usually controlled her baser urges better

than this but for some reason she totally blew it this time. Like Veronica, she almost broke her neck trying to get a glimpse of her incredibly late blind date.

Any oxygen in her lungs evaporated as instantaneously as a drop of water on a scorching desert rock.

David was gorgeous. Drop-dead gorgeous in fact.

Apparently noticing Sabrina's stunned look, Veronica leaned close and whispered, "I told you. My Wesley has exceptional taste."

Sabrina shot her a disdainful look. "The jury's still out," she muttered.

David paused at their table, apologizing profusely and then introductions were made.

It had been a very long time since anyone had waltzed into a room and blown Sabrina away like this guy did. Maybe she'd just been lonely for far too long. Whatever the case, the tide turned and the night suddenly had the makings of a great evening. She'd have to thank her friend later. Much later.

Dinner and dancing with expensive wine and intelligent conversation were enough to make any girl happy for a few hours. But by 1 a.m., Sabrina was ready to go. And her hurry had nothing to do with the food or the place or the time.

It was David.

She hadn't been this determined to take a man home with her in far too long to recall.

Veronica and Wesley waved goodbye as they loaded into their taxi. David didn't need to hail a cab because he had his own limo. He gave the driver Sabrina's address before powering up the privacy shield.

At thirty-two, and well experienced in the ways of the world Sabrina was not usually this easily impressed. But she had to admit, this guy had pushed all the right buttons.

She wanted him.

"Would you like a nightcap?" He gestured to the minibar as the luxurious vehicle smoothly rolled away from the curb.

Sabrina moved her head slowly from side to side as she slid off first one shoe and then the other. There was only one thing she wanted right now.

As if he'd been waiting all night for that single cue, David loosened his tie and shouldered out of his jacket. He ushered Sabrina down onto the seat and spread open her heavy faux fur coat. He kissed her nose and then her eyes before placing his lips firmly over hers. The kiss was slow, thorough and incredibly sexy. The fire, by contrast, did not start out slow and easy, it blazed instantly and roared out of control, making her greedy for more.

He kissed his way down her throat and to the

cleavage revealed by the low-cut dress. He smoothed his hands over her thighs and hips, and then he started to do things that drove her completely mad.

Within sixty seconds of his first kiss, he had her coming fast and furiously and he hadn't even unzipped his trousers.

She came twice before they reached her building, David using nothing more than his skilled touch, his equally masterful kiss. He sent his driver home and they kissed some more as they entered her building. She didn't remember how they managed the four flights to her floor, only the feel of his mouth and hands on her body. She couldn't remember when she'd enjoyed kissing so much. There was something so enticing about his mouth.

Somehow they reached her apartment and she fumbled for the key. Once they were on the other side of that door, a desperate race to get naked started. By the time they fell onto the bed together, she was rushing toward climax yet again at the mere thought of finally having him inside her. She jerked open a drawer in her bedside table, fishing for a condom. He ripped open the package and slid on the protection sending her heart rate into triple digits just watching his hand slide over his hard, fully erect member.

He moved over her and kissed her long and

deep before nudging firmly between her thighs. She'd almost forgotten the incredible ecstasy of that first moment of penetration. He pushed his way inside and held very still until they'd both caught their breath.

Then he started the frenzy all over again with his hands. The way he touched every place that longed for attention without her having to say a word was indescribably hedonistic, especially with that incredible sense of fullness where she needed it most. He massaged, licked and nuzzled her body while keeping his hips perfectly still. Every muscle in her body responded to his touch, begged for more.

And then he moved. Flexed those lean, powerful hips in that age-old rhythm that sent her over the edge in two deep thrusts.

Hours later, when he collapsed beside her she'd come no less than five times. A record.

Completely exhausted and utterly sated for the first time in what felt like forever, she drifted in and out of sleep. David slept like the dead beside her. Not that she could blame him. He'd worked hard to give her those five lovely orgasms.

Any man who could do that deserved plenty of rest.

She got up and went to the kitchen in search of a bottle of wine. Standing naked at the fridge, she peered inside to see if there was anything that struck her fancy in the way of a snack. She grabbed the block of cheese and a bunch of grapes and prepared a small platter of snacks. Her lover might not wake up, but she was starved.

With her bounty on a tray, she wandered back to the bedroom. She set the tray on the table by the window and then curled into the chair next to it. As she sipped her wine, she studied the man in her bed. She didn't know that much about him except that his name was David Hedrick and he worked on Wall Street. Unlike Veronica, she wasn't looking for commitment and certainly not for a husband, so no other details were especially essential.

The dim glow from the lamp on the bedside table provided just enough illumination for her to appreciate his numerous assets. Her gaze slid over his tight buttocks and along his long legs. No. She didn't need a husband or even a steady boyfriend. But sex, well, that was another story. She'd forgotten just how much she enjoyed it.

It had been too long.

The image of another man loomed in her head and she pushed it aside. She told herself her long abstinence had nothing to do with him, but she wasn't entirely convincing. But he was in the past, over, gone. She wasn't one to dwell in the past.

She tipped her glass and emptied it in one long swallow. Sleep tugged at her, but she ignored it and poured herself another glass of wine. She intended to have at least two more before she let herself sleep. Otherwise she was sure to dream about that past she so badly wanted to forget.

Maybe that was what tonight's desperate love-making had been about.

No, she argued. Tonight with David hadn't been about the past. Tonight had been about her needs as a woman. Nothing else.

The telephone rang. She heard the annoying clatter from the living room. She'd long ago turned off the ringer to the bedside extension. If work called, they used her cell phone, not her landline.

She stood, grabbed the bottle of wine and trudged off to the living room to answer the call. If it was Veronica, then Sabrina might just have to kill her.

After a long swallow directly from the bottle, Sabrina grabbed the receiver. "This better be good," she threatened.

Silence.

Well, hell. "Hello?"

More of that thick silence.

She hated when this happened. When she started to hang up, she head the sound…a whisper of air as if someone had taken a breath.

Dammit.

"I know you're there. If you don't want me to hear you, then hold your breath."

She waited three more beats before she hung up.

A quick glance at the clock confirmed her suspicions. 3:30 a.m. The call came at that same hour every time.

And she knew it was *him*. She couldn't prove it, of course. But she knew.

Damn him.

Eric Drake. *The Dragon*.

The mere thought of his name sent shivers chasing one another over her skin.

She had worked hard to put him behind her, to get over him, but the wound had never completely closed. She'd let him so deep inside her that she wasn't sure it was humanly possible to completely evict him.

He'd been her Interpol counterpart, her lover, her everything…and that had been a mistake.

One she would never make again.

She headed back to bed, sleep and the effects of the wine clawing at her now. She surrendered to it, let it push thoughts of *him* from her mind.

The shrill ring of the phone split the air once more.

Swearing, she rolled over and snatched up the receiver. "What?" If this was him… Why the hell did he do this? Why didn't he just leave her alone?

"Sabrina?"

Oh, hell. Her sister.

"Leslie, sorry about that. I thought you were someone else." Then she remembered the time. She sat bolt upright, the haze of sleep and wine dissolving instantly. "What's wrong?"

"It's Mom. You need to meet me at the hospital."

And just like that Sabrina's great night was over.

CHAPTER FOUR

THERE WAS SOMETHING about the medicinal smell of a hospital that made Sabrina think of running away. It wasn't that the people inside the hospital were sick or dying, which, of course, was depressing enough. No, she was pretty sure it was more likely because for as long as she could remember, her mother had required regular hospital admissions. Growing up, she and her sister had spent many nights holding vigil at their mother's hospital bedside.

Not due to any physical ailment. Nope, her mother had been and still was, to some degree, a hypochondriac. Janelle Fox could suck the very life out of other human beings with her neediness. Everything was all about her.

"She's really sick this time, Sabrina."

Sabrina didn't doubt her sister's assessment, but somehow, standing here in this hospital in Kansas after all these years of watching their mother pull this crap, it was hard to be sympathetic.

Leslie, her only sibling, had always defended their mother. Maybe because she was the oldest and somehow felt it was her job. Whatever the reason, Sabrina was the third wheel in this relationship. Especially since their father had passed away.

"What's the diagnosis?" Sabrina hated that her skepticism showed, but, hey, she'd scarcely had any sleep.

Leslie Fanning shook her blond head in slow contempt. "I don't know why you even came." She had the same hazel eyes and tall, lean physique as Sabrina, but their personalities heralded from opposite universes.

Sabrina shrugged. "I don't know why you even called me." She leaned against the cold, white wall and folded her arms over her chest. She wasn't going to take any holier-than-thou crap from her sister this time. The episode three months ago had been the last straw.

"You are unbelievable, do you know that?" Leslie hissed. She glanced around the corridor to make sure no one had heard her hushed outburst. "Our mother could be on her deathbed and you wouldn't care."

Sabrina rubbed her eyes with her thumb and forefinger. This was so ridiculous. The same old melodrama they'd played out a dozen times before. "You don't know how I feel, Leslie, so don't pretend you do."

"I know that I'm the one who lives here." She moved closer so she could keep her voice down, but that didn't keep her outrage from oozing from every pore of her skin. "I'm the one who takes care of her needs, week in and week out. While you're off in New York being *you* and without a care as to what anyone else needs."

Sabrina looked at her sister, really looked at her for the first time in a long while. She did look tired, and older…older than her thirty-seven years. Maybe Sabrina wasn't giving her sister full credit here.

"You're right. I'm not here. I don't know how it really is. I can only go by what I see when this stuff happens."

Leslie leaned against the wall, the heavy sigh she exhaled confirmation of her fatigue. "She does really well for a while. Then something goes wrong." She tucked a handful of blond hair behind her ear. "Something little, like running out of dish soap for the dishwasher. Any little thing. And she starts ranting about how she can't remember anything and that she must have Alzheimer's. Then the drinking starts. She calls me all hours of the day and night. *I—*" she thumped her chest "— have to go take care of her. *I* have to leave my husband and kids and go stay the night with Mom or rush her to the E.R. That's how it is."

Sabrina hadn't really considered all that taking

care of her mom on a regular basis entailed. Possibly she'd oversimplified the situation to assuage her own conscience for far too long.

"I'm sorry, Leslie." For the first time in a very long time, Sabrina hugged her sister.

"I have the kids to think of, you know." Leslie dabbed at her eyes. "Ryan's in high school now. Carly's in middle school. It's tough to take care of Mom when she goes on her binges."

Sabrina had left Kansas immediately after college. Leslie had stayed, gone to college nearby, spending every weekend being the dutiful daughter. After graduation, she'd married and settled close by. In reality, Leslie had never really left home.

Sabrina prepared for a fight. "Maybe it's time we talked about a home."

Outrage flashed in her sister's eyes. "That's perfect, Sabrina. Leave it to you to suggest putting our mother away."

Fourteen years. Sabrina had been gone from Kansas for fourteen years and still her sister could make her feel like pond scum with a few words.

Sabrina felt her own fury kick in. "You know what, Leslie? You're not going to make me feel guilty for following my dream. You and Dad and everyone else allowed Mother to get to this point. No one ever stood up to her the way I tried to." She shoved a hand through her hair, frustrated as much with herself as with her sister. "Was it easier to just let her do what she would? Like an errant child? Pretend it doesn't exist and it'll go away?"

"You wouldn't know, would you?" Leslie lashed back. "You're never here."

Sabrina threw up her hands. "You know what? I'm not here now, either."

With that, she walked out of the hospital.

The call had come just before four that morning. Sabrina had awakened David and sent him on his way and then spent nearly an hour on the phone trying to get a flight. By the time she'd packed, sat through the wait at Newark, made the flight and gotten a rental car for the drive from the airport, she was totally exhausted. She hadn't had one wink of sleep and she'd driven all the way from Kansas City without so much as stopping for a cup of coffee. Only to find out her mother had almost died of alcohol poisoning for the sixth time in the last five years. There was a message in there. Wasn't anybody listening?

The woman had a problem. She should be in rehab.

Sabrina stormed all the way to her rental car before she stopped and took a breath.

She couldn't just leave.

Leslie would never forgive her. And despite their difference of opinion where their mother was concerned, Sabrina did love both of them. Fiercely.

Maybe she hadn't been a very good sister or daughter or aunt. She thought of Leslie's two kids. She saw them every year at Christmas, and that was about it. But that didn't make her a monster. She was busy. She couldn't share anything about her work with her family. Her personal life in New York was a world away from their small-town way of living here in Kansas. What were they supposed to talk about? The truth was, they really had nothing in common except DNA.

And sometimes that just wasn't enough.

Like now.

No matter. Leslie was right about one thing— Sabrina wasn't here for their mother like she was. Maybe it was time she tried to do her part, whether they wanted her to or not.

First, she needed a phone book. Stopping at a local diner, she used her cell phone and called every facility within a hundred miles. The one she liked best was only thirty minutes away and offered the very services their mother needed— comfort and supervision, along with intensive counseling. The administrator had said that if Sabrina could be there by five she would give her the grand tour. The only problem was, she needed Leslie with her on this.

That wouldn't be easy.

LESLIE PACED back and forth in front of the door to their mother's room. She looked up when Sabrina approached.

"I was afraid you wouldn't come back."

Of course her sister would think the worst. Someone in this relationship had to be the bad guy, had to be the black sheep of the family, and it had traditionally been Sabrina.

"Is she doing okay?" Sabrina asked glancing at the closed door.

Leslie nodded. "She's better. The doctor stopped in and assured me that she would be fine." She exhaled a heavy breath. "This time." She leveled her gaze on Sabrina's. "He said the same thing you've been saying all along. If we don't stop the binges, she'll…"

The pain in her sister's eyes had Sabrina wrapping her arms around her and holding her tight for the second time in scarcely half a dozen hours. "I know. I know."

Now or never.

Sabrina pulled back first. "Look, if we leave right now there's something I can show you that might help."

Leslie glanced at the door, clearly hesitant about leaving. "She's sleeping. I…suppose it would be okay if we left for a little while."

"Great. Come on."

Sabrina stopped by the nurse's desk and gave the duty nurse her cell number.

"Where are we going?" Leslie finally asked when they loaded into Sabrina's car.

"You'll see." Sabrina was almost afraid that if she told Leslie before they were on the road that she'd balk. She wasn't about to take the risk.

The drive took exactly thirty minutes, during which time they discussed Leslie's home renovations and the coming holiday. She asked about Sabrina's work, specifically which countries she'd visited in the past couple of months. Sometimes, like now, Sabrina longed to share the whole truth with her. But, of course, she couldn't.

After the tour, Sabrina thanked the administrator for taking the time to show them around on such short notice. The facility housed every amenity any specialized hospital would, but also had a comfortable, homey atmosphere. It was exactly what their mother needed.

When they'd gotten back on the highway headed in the direction of the hospital, she broached the subject with her sister.

"So, what'd you think?"

Leslie didn't answer right away, giving Sabrina's tension a chance to ratchet a little higher.

Any other time she might have found the moment amusing. She faced death on every assignment. Yet here she sat, worried sick about what her sister would think of the facility she'd chosen.

"I think it's really great." Leslie made no attempts to hide her surprise. "In fact, I'm sitting here now asking myself why I hadn't already looked into this."

Sabrina resisted the urge to shout *yes*. Now for the next hurdle. "For the last ten years," she began, bracing for her sister's reaction, "you've taken really good care of Mom. You've been there for her whenever anything happened, whenever she needed you. Now it's my turn."

"What're you saying?"

"I'll take care of the full cost of the facility. It won't be a problem." Sabrina's fingers tightened on the steering wheel as if it were the butt of a weapon, but somehow she doubted it would protect her from the hellfire missiles her sister might launch.

"Are you serious?"

Afraid to believe that would be the worst of Leslie's reaction, Sabrina hesitantly glanced in her sister's direction. "Totally serious."

"Tell me again what it is you do in New York?"

Sabrina had to laugh. She'd been working in New York for years, and this was apparently the first time her sister had considered that she might command a handsome salary.

"You're not doing anything dangerous are you? I mean, should Mom and I be worried?"

Sabrina tensed at the change in Leslie's tone. She should have seen that one coming. So she took the only out she could. "Of course not. Why would I be involved in anything dangerous?"

"Good." Leslie sighed as if glad to have that weight off her chest. "So, is there a man in your life?"

Talk about a subject change. "I guess you could say I'm still playing the field." Sabrina gave herself a mental pat on the back for dodging that one.

Unfortunately, Leslie saw right through her. "Surely there's someone. You don't want to talk about him?"

The name that rushed to the tip of Sabrina's tongue had her wanting to bite it off. She blinked away the image that accompanied the name. She would not, absolutely would not, go there. *He* was gone…forever.

"You hesitated! There is someone. Come on, don't cop out on me like this. We're bonding!"

Sabrina knew she would regret this, but her sister was right—they *were* bonding. "There was someone, but that was a long time ago. We haven't seen each other in two years." She refused to think his name, much less say it. She'd made that mistake at 3:30 a.m. this morning. "I guess I still haven't gotten completely over him."

It was the first time she'd ever admitted that out loud.

"You're sure there's no going back and making amends?"

There was the major difference between the two of them. Sabrina knew the way things were in the real world, her sister, well, she was still in Kansas.

"I'm afraid there's no going back."

SABRINA DECIDED TO SPEND the night at her sister's home. She needed to catch up on how things were going with the kids, and she wasn't on call this weekend. She and Leslie could fill out the papers for their mother's admission to the assisted living facility. There would be more bonding time and Sabrina would get a good night's sleep. Everyone benefited.

But the great sleep she'd looked forward to wouldn't come. She lay in bed staring at the ceiling part of the time and fought the covers the rest.

She thought about her sister's nice, neat home at the end of a lovely cul-de-sac. Two beautiful kids. Great husband. And the dog. Maybe Sabrina was missing something by avoiding the whole commitment gig.

Not!

She'd thought about committing…once. And look where that had gotten her—her heart damaged and fear of getting anywhere near commitment ever again.

Well, all right, maybe she wasn't afraid. Secret agents who narrowly escaped death on a regular basis weren't afraid of anything.

Resistant. That was a better description of what she was when it came to getting *involved* with a man on that level. Resistant.

It wasn't as if there were no hope whatsoever. She was only thirty-two, for goodness sake. There would be other opportunities, other men.

Like David.

She smiled. Oh yeah. Now there was a handy guy to have around. Great sex. Not only did he know all the right spots, he didn't mind taking the time to make sure he gave them ample attention.

Definitely handy. Amazing sex.

A grinding sound dragged her attention to the bedside table. Her cell phone lit up and vibrated across the top.

If this was Protocol, they'd just have to consider that she was in Kansas.

She checked the caller ID display before she flipped the phone open. Private call. Dammit. She knew exactly what this meant. "Fox."

Silence.

"Who the hell is this?"

Then she heard a shallow intake of air, just enough to give away the presence of someone on the other end of the line.

She told the caller where to get off, closed the

phone and slapped it down on the table. First thing Monday, she was taking her phone in to Big Hugh for a full analysis. She would find the source of those damned calls.

Pulling the cover back up around her, she lay there and fumed. No way would she be able to sleep now.

She should never have trusted *him*. Eric Drake had been a mistake from day one. A monumental mistake.

Marx had introduced them. *Drake, this is our Sabrina Fox.*

Our Sabrina Fox. Sabrina didn't know to this day what precisely Marx had seen in her, besides her linguistic skills and her uncanny ability to fit into any given situation almost like an actress. But he'd wooed her into the intelligence-gathering section of IT&PA. She vaguely recalled something he'd said about her keen ability to focus so intently.

Eventually Marx had insisted that, desk work or not, being a part of that special organization required other skills, as well. Much to her surprise, she had taken to her marksmanship training like a duck to water. Hand-to-hand combat, shadowing a target—anything tossed her way, she could handle it.

Her first field op, an intelligence gathering mission, had gone south in a hurry. Later Marx had praised her quick thinking and ability to handle herself in a dicey situation. She'd been in the field ever since. And he'd personally walked her through the emotional changes every step of the way.

It wasn't until later that she'd been teamed up with Drake. That was when she'd learned that the Dragon had been watching her all that time...and more. She'd discovered that Drake and Marx had pegged her that first year she was with the UN as someone they wanted on the IT&PA team.

She had been handpicked to serve her country.

That part wasn't a mistake. She was wholly dedicated to her work and damn proud to be part of the team. It was only *him* that she regretted.

Sabrina had, of course, heard of the legendary Dragon. She just hadn't expected that he'd heard of her, and she definitely hadn't anticipated ending up his counterpart.

You're the perfect agent, Fox, Drake had told her. *Absolutely beautiful and entirely dangerous.*

He'd waltzed into her life and stolen her heart. For him, it had been as easy as a smile and a wink. His killer good looks and vast charm had been irresistible. She'd fallen hard and fast.

You're mine, Sabrina. You'll always be mine.

She squeezed her eyes shut against the memory of those whispered words. She would not do this.

It had taken far too long to train herself not to grieve the loss. She couldn't let him haunt her like this.

He was gone…forever.

CHAPTER FIVE

SABRINA EMERGED from the cab around six on Sunday evening. She traveled frequently. Oftentimes she was gone for a week to ten days. But somehow the last thirty-six or so hours felt like a year.

"I love this city." She drew in a deep, calming breath of cool air and turned all the way around on the sidewalk, admiring the entire block. She felt exactly like Dorothy in *The Wizard of Oz*; she definitely wasn't in Kansas anymore.

She was home.

On 36th Street in Manhattan's Garment District.

Thank God.

She hustled up the steps and used her key to unlock the main entrance to her building. "I love this building," she muttered as the door closed behind her.

After a check of her mailbox she made quick work of the four flights of stairs up to her apartment. She paused at the door and slid the key into the lock. She was so glad to be home.

Inside, she dropped her overnight bag on the floor, leaned against the closed door and exhaled a mighty breath. She loved her apartment. It might not be three thousand square feet like her sister's modern ranch-style home and it might not have two kids or a dog or a husband loafing around inside, but it was home and she adored every square inch.

As if her reflexes had only just then kicked into gear, Sabrina froze. The tiny hairs on the back of her neck stood on end.

Every instinct screamed at her that something was off.

She eased closer to the coat closet, wrapped her fingers around the doorknob and held her breath as she turned it. Her senses alert for the first sign of movement or sound, she reached into the specially designed interior pocket of the coat she wore for social occasions and retrieved the .22 she kept stashed there. No one ever expected to find a gun inside a faux fur coat.

Adopting a fire-ready posture, she stayed close to the wall and moved around the perimeter of the room toward the bedroom. She surveyed the kitchen as she passed the bar that separated it from her living room. There were few options for hiding in her kitchen.

Next she checked the bathroom, which was wide-open. Her heart kicked into a slightly faster rhythm as she whipped the shower curtain back.

Empty.

No place left to hide except the bedroom.

At the partially closed door to her bedroom, she paused to listen. Nothing. Not a single sound. Still, something was wrong. She could feel it.

Readying for battle, she took a deep breath before bursting through the door.

Only to find her bedroom empty.

Rumpled bed. Clothes on the floor. The closet door stood open, with more clothes spewing from it. And nothing else.

She relaxed marginally. Checked behind the door, under the bed. Nothing.

Deep breath. Okay. What the hell was wrong with her? Her instincts were usually way more on target than this.

And then she saw the problem.

The bedroom window was open. The sheer curtains fluttered on the crisp breeze that floated in at that precise moment.

She trembled as the cold air penetrated the clothes she wore.

No way had she opened the window and forgotten it. Not in December. She was certain the window had been closed when she left.

Sabrina closed the window and searched her entire apartment, every drawer, every shelf. Nothing was missing, nothing had been touched as far as she could determine. Yet someone had been there. She would need Big Hugh and Trainer to come in and do a sweep for bugs.

The idea that *he* might have been in her apartment made her tremble. Stop it, she ordered. Someone had been here all right, but it wouldn't have been him.

Why was he suddenly on her mind all the time? She couldn't shake him. Dammit.

Maybe she was just tired. She leaned against the window in her living room and stared out at the snow that had started to fall. She liked the snow. It made everything look bright and clean. God's gift in the winter, that was what her father had always said. *A little something to get us through the dark winter nights.* She liked remembering the little things such as that about him. He'd been that kind of man. Not the least bit arrogant or boastful. Just a kind person, completely selfless, full of wisdom and compassion for all he encountered in his life.

Why couldn't she pick a guy like that?

No, she had to be drawn to the dangerous ones. The men who took what they wanted and never looked back.

Just her dumb luck to fall in love with one.

Enough.

That call last night had her on edge. It was the first time she'd gotten the anonymous call two nights in a row. Two mornings, she amended, since they came around three-thirty.

She told herself it couldn't be *him*.

But she always wondered.

Somehow she had to find a way to banish Eric Drake from her head once and for all.

And she had to find out who the hell was playing with her head. The calls…the window… all of it was building toward something she couldn't quite see just yet.

Three brisk raps on the door to her apartment sent her pulse back into overdrive.

Sabrina silently railed at herself as she crossed the room. She had to get a handle on this whole situation.

What had happened to her calm, quiet personal life?

She checked the peephole in her door and jerked back at what she saw on the other side. Not what…who.

Colin Ledger.

What was he doing here?

More memories she'd just as soon not recall vied for her attention. Ledger had taken over as her Interpol counterpart after Drake…left. She'd actually worked with both to some degree. The two men had always carried on this competition as to who was the best.

Funny that Ledger should show up at her door just now.

She stowed her weapon and opened the door.

She produced the requisite smile, but even that didn't stop her big mouth from echoing her thought. "Ledger, what the hell are you doing here?"

"Nice to see you, as well, Fox."

No matter how much time he spent jockeying around the world, his accent remained impeccable. The Queen herself would surely approve.

Sabrina opened the door wider in welcome. "I was about to have a glass of wine. Would you care to join me?" Actually, it wasn't so surprising that he was here, she admitted. He spent about as much time in the U.S. as he did in his home country. The totally odd thing was that he hadn't called before showing up. Brits rarely committed that sort of social faux pas. Or maybe it was just the thing with the window and the frequency of her anonymous calls that had her looking for hidden agendas tonight.

"That would be lovely." He crossed the threshold and tugged off his jacket at the same time noting the coat and bag she'd left on the floor.

"I'll take that," she said as she reached for his leather jacket that had likely been imported from someplace exotic and expensive. She grabbed her own coat, as well.

As she put away the coats away, she ticked off the possible reasons for his visit. She presumed it wasn't personal since she had made it clear that she would not be getting involved with anymore spy types. Even if she was a spy type. She preferred safe men nowadays. Wall Street guys or advertising execs. Like David.

"Have a seat." She gestured to her sofa. "I'll get the wine."

"Perhaps I might be of some assistance," he offered politely.

She held up her hands stop-sign fashion. "Sit. I've got it under control."

In the kitchen, she filled two stemmed glasses with the merlot she preferred. This visit couldn't be about business, she decided. Protocol would have called her if something between IT&PA and Interpol had come up.

Maybe he was in the city, whether for business or pleasure, and was simply bored.

That had to be it.

Sure, they'd had a couple of dates about a year ago. She'd sworn off handsome, dangerous men, but they'd been in London together on a mission and she'd…well, she'd gotten a little caught up in the moment.

They'd kissed, just one foolish kiss. He'd tried several times after that to rekindle that brief fire, but she just couldn't go there. They'd worked together a couple of times since, and the issue hadn't come up again.

It was over. Behind them.

As handsome as he was, as charming as he was,

she would not end up in bed with Colin Ledger.
Not for all the houses, kids and dogs on the planet.

"Here we go," she announced too cheerily as
she breezed back into the living room.

He accepted the glass she offered. "Splendid."

Sabrina took a chair across the coffee table
from his position on the sofa. "What brings you
to New York?" She had to know. In her experience
with Ledger, cutting straight to the chase was his
preference as well.

He tasted his wine and made a sound of
approval. That he made her shiver with nothing
more than that deep, throaty sound launched a
streak of annoyance straight across her brow. Why
hadn't she noticed before now that she had a
headache beginning in that exact spot?

He was handsome, sexy, charming. Boyish
dimples and thick sandy blond hair. Deep brown
eyes that looked like melted chocolate. But he was
way off limits. Thank God she'd met David the
other night, or she might just be desperate enough...

"Last-minute holiday shopping."

She blinked. Studied that handsome face. His
answer was a lie.

She'd had extensive training in spotting untruths
the same as he had. He knew better than to lie to her.

"No, really, Ledger, why are you here?"

He set his glass aside and pondered her with a
bemused expression, making whatever was on his

mind unreadable. "Really, Fox, you do need to stop being so suspicious of everyone. I am here to shop."

"They don't have department stores in London?"

He picked up his glass and swirled his wine for a moment before answering. "If you want the truth, Fox, I had a meeting with your director and while I was here I wanted to see you. And, yes, there are lots of lovely shops in London but none of them offers what I'm looking for just now."

Her mind zeroed in on his significant admission. A meeting with Director Marx? "What kind of meeting?"

He lifted an eyebrow in surprise. "You know I can't divulge the nature of my business with Marx."

Her instincts must have been fuzzy; otherwise she would have sworn Ledger was doing some heavy-duty tap dancing to avoid simply telling her the truth. She sat her glass on the table in front of her and scrutinized him a little longer before asking, "Official?"

He nodded. "Of course. Except for the part about coming to see you."

"Ledger."

"Fox." He eased forward to the edge of his seat, lessening the distance between them. "It's Christmas time. You're not going to deny a man his one Christmas wish, are you?"

Now that was a jab below the belt. This was a new low, even for a charming Brit.

"We've talked about this before," she countered. Why did he bring it up again?

He lifted his glass in a little salute. "And I keep hoping you'll change your mind." He downed a hefty swallow.

"Marx thinks you work too much, you know."

"You and Director Marx talked about me?" Now she was pissed off. Ledger had no right talking about her to her boss or vice versa. Marx already knew about her fiasco two years ago. She definitely didn't want him thinking she'd slipped up again and gotten involved with her counterpart. Even if she *almost* had.

Ledger flashed her that charming smile that probably got him laid more often than not. "It wasn't intentional, I assure you. His secretary had given him the note regarding your trip to Kansas and I just happened to be in his office at the time. How is your mother, by the way?"

"She's fine." Now Sabrina couldn't stop obsessing about what Marx may or may not have said about her.

Ledger nodded. "I'm pleased to hear that. Nothing else was said about you, I promise." He placed his glass on the table next to his chair. "You do work too hard. Everyone knows that about you, Fox."

"Somehow it's difficult to find anything you say reassuring, Ledger. We both make our living with deception and illusion. Nothing is ever as simple as it seems. Why don't you tell me the real reason you're here?"

Ledger regarded her a moment before responding. "I'm thinking of making a move, Fox. IT&PA is working overtime to lure me away from Interpol."

Now there was a shocker. "Are you seriously considering the move?" Not only was his announcement a surprise, it would surely be one for the record books. Interpol agents didn't defect to NSA. It just wasn't done.

There had to be an extremely compelling reason.

He gave a little noncommittal lift of his shoulders. "I'm seriously considering it, yes."

"What position?" That had to be the key. Somehow the realization had her poised on the edge of her seat. This was the part that affected her somehow. The realization was abruptly crystal clear. That was why he was here.

"Deputy director."

In seven years, IT&PA had never had a deputy director. Marx ran the show, and everyone else followed his orders. This would be a big deal.

"So you'd be my boss."

"Yes, in theory. The change would be purely executive in nature. Agents such as yourself would continue to do your job just as you have in the past. The only difference is that I would serve as the overseer of field operations while Marx stuck to policy and coordination with the other agencies."

Oh, yes, megachanges. Big Hugh, Trainer, Angie, none of them was going to like this. It wasn't that Ledger wasn't a nice guy, but he was coming from outside to take over. That was always a painful transition. Although, she had to admit, there wasn't one of them who would want the deputy spot, Still, to bring in an outsider was touchy.

"When would this change become official?"

"As soon as I've given Marx an answer."

"You're waiting for Interpol to come up with an equivalent offer?"

"No. Interpol has given their blessing to the move."

Okay, she was officially stumped. "I don't get it then, why don't you just say yes?"

"I need to know the answer to one question before I can make my decision."

"Where you'd live? Are you checking out the housing market?" He did say he was here to do a little shopping.

"Nothing that simple, I'm afraid."

She waited for him to continue because she sure as hell couldn't figure out what had him hesitating.

"If I accept the position that means there is no chance for you and I. Fraternization, and all that poppycock."

As deputy director, he would be her boss. "Oh."

He inclined his head, assessed her with those brown eyes. "You see my dilemma, then?"

She didn't, really. "I thought we'd decided that keeping our relationship strictly professional was the best for all concerned."

Maybe she was the one who didn't get it. They'd had that one kiss. A couple of dates. But she'd realized before it was too late that she could not go there again.

"You decided," he countered softly. "You know how I feel, Sabrina. You can't possibly not know. I would very much like to pursue this connection between us."

She couldn't say he wasn't persistent. "As flattered as I am, Ledger, I can't do it. I would like very much to remain friends, but that's the best I can do."

The subtle shift in his eyes told her he wasn't pleased with her decision. "Because of Drake?"

The name resonated through her like the echo of a gun blast. She suppressed the resulting quake. "He's part of the reason," she admitted. "It's too complicated."

She wanted that to be enough, but evidently it wasn't.

"I don't want you to make a final decision tonight. Think about it and let me know in a few days."

"Ledger, I—"

"Please, Sabrina," he urged. "Do this for me. Think about it for a day or two, and then let's talk again. I'll be in the city for several more days."

What was she supposed to say to that? "All right." Regret that she hadn't stuck by her guns immediately rushed through her. Putting off the inevitable would only give him false hope.

His relief was palpable. "Splendid." He stood. "I should be going."

She pushed to her feet and followed him to the door. She retrieved his coat.

"It was nice to see you again, Ledger." Again, she regretted her choice in words. But it *was* nice to see him. She liked him. She just couldn't love him. And that was what he wanted. Colin Ledger, spy or not, was one of those guys who wanted to keep his secret life and have all the other perks, too. A wife, children, the house. The whole works.

Before turning to go, he peered deeply into her eyes. She wondered if he hoped to see some emotion shining there that would give him something to hang on to. They were friends. That was all she felt. He needed to see that.

"Good night, Sabrina." He leaned down and pressed a soft kiss to her cheek.

And then he was gone.

She closed the door and engaged the dead bolts.

Suddenly, she felt even more exhausted. What next?

She shuffled across the room to look out the window. On the street below, she watched Ledger stride confidently toward the car waiting for him.

A thin layer of snow had already covered the street and sidewalk, slowly turning it a pristine white. She wished the emotions churning around inside her right now could so easily be covered.

What the hell was going on? Some invisible thread holding her life stable had somehow became unraveled. She had to get back on track. Regain control.

Tomorrow was another day…and it damn sure had to be better.

She turned out the lights and crawled into bed. God, she was so tired. If she were lucky, there wouldn't be any dreams. Just a long night of un-interrupted slumber.

Tomorrow she could look at all of this more rationally.

Somehow she would get her point across to Ledger that friends was all she wanted to be.

No more mistakes for her.

As she drifted off to sleep, she felt *him* trying to intrude as surely as he did with those calls. *If the caller was him.* And if it was him, it wouldn't do her any good to take her phone in for analysis. He was way too smart to be traced.

Way too handsome for his own good.

And way too lethal for her good.

Drake. Eric Drake. The man who'd stolen her heart three years ago, then crushed it just one year later.

The Dragon.

She wasn't even sure he was still alive. For all she knew, he could be dead and buried somewhere without a soul to mourn him.

The same way she would likely end up at this rate.

Completely alone.

CHAPTER SIX

ON MONDAY MORNING, Sabrina donned her snow boots. Four inches of snow had fallen overnight. The city looked as if it had been covered in chic white rabbit fur. Luxurious and pristine.

Her black skirt hit mid-calf, the black sweater fit snugly with a high collar that accentuated the length of her neck. She pulled on her coat and gloves, then took extra time to wind the scarf smartly around her throat and shoulders.

Snagging her briefcase, she was out of there.

The sky was clear, the air crisp and cold. Sabrina shivered as she descended the steps down to the sidewalk. Even the bare tree limbs had managed to serve as shelves for last night's snow dump. Window boxes were loaded with the white stuff, the occasional colorful winter blossom poking out its delicate head.

Her sister had called to let her know that she would be dropping off their mother's paperwork and the check Sabrina had left with the administrator of the assisted living facility today. If all worked out as it should, Janelle could move in within two weeks. Sabrina had promised to visit at least every other month.

Her sister was right; she needed to reconnect with her family. Their mother wasn't getting any younger, and Leslie's kids were growing up. It was the right thing to do for all concerned.

Once she reached 5th Avenue the sidewalks were in better shape, making for a less hazardous journey. Ten blocks to 46th and then over to 1st Avenue. As cold as it was, she enjoyed the winter scene. Things looked different decorated with snow.

She imagined that her love of Christmas and snow would seem strange to anyone who learned the true nature of her occupation. The fact that her work required that she take the enemy's life from time to time didn't make her a brutal person. She simply did what she had to do, like any good soldier when sent out to fight a war. And this was a war. The enemy came in all shapes and sizes now and from too many sources to name. Preparation and stead-fastness were the keys to keeping the country safe.

As a college student back in Kansas, the idea of becoming an intervention specialist was the farthest thing from her mind. She hadn't known such an occupation existed. She and her col-leagues intervened in situations otherwise unsal-vageable with as little collateral damage as possible. Surgical strikes. Oftentimes the assignment was one of assessment or data collection—in other words, plain old spying—rather than something confrontational.

Her ability to fit in with Europeans as well as Americans in most any setting, as well as her language skills, was essential to her work at IT&PA. Despite the fact that much of the terror threats these days appeared to spring from the Middle East, the truth was that more often than not the perpetrators were imbedded in Europe or right here in the U.S., making her European language specialty invaluable.

Still, if Director Marx had told her on their first meeting that she would become a trained killer, Sabrina felt certain she would have laughed and then walked out of his office. Marx had been far savvier than that. He'd eased her into the full scope of training one level at a time. By the time she'd reached the weaponry phase, the concept had seemed totally logical.

She enjoyed the highest security clearance available to anyone who wasn't president of the country. The secrecy was the only part of her work that became disconcerting from time to time. Like when her sister had questioned her. There simply was no way to answer her questions without sounding suspicious. Sabrina just didn't see how Angie did it. Keeping her husband and kids in the dark had to be far more difficult than lying to one's sister and mother.

Lying. She didn't generally consider her half truths and concocted explanations as lies. But that was what they were.

She shook off the self-reflection. She was supposed to be putting all this emotional stuff behind her this morning. All in all, her weekend hadn't been half-bad.

Except for the calls.

She'd gotten another one at three-thirty this morning. Sleep after that had been impossible. But since she'd crashed at eight, she'd had plenty of rest in spite of the early wake-up call. Her apartment had needed a good cleaning anyway. She'd even schlepped down to the basement and done laundry, including her bed sheets. Washing away David once and for all. She probably wouldn't ever see him again.

It was better this way. No strings.

A burst of adrenaline roared through her veins, sending those tiny hairs to attention for the second time in less than twenty-four hours.

She whipped around to look behind her, her fingers itching to go for the weapon in her purse.

No one was there.

She exhaled a heavy breath that turned to fog in the cold air. What was with all this paranoia? She pivoted and started forward again. *Stupid, Sabrina. Really stupid.*

She took half a dozen more steps, and the

undeniable crunch of frozen snow sounded behind her.

She wheeled around. Caught a glimpse of a dark figure disappearing between two buildings.

Now that was not paranoia.

"Gotcha."

Breaking into a dead run, her right hand jammed into her purse, she darted into the same alley. She'd been right. Someone was following her.

He had a good head start, but she was gaining.

Her fingers wrapped around the butt of her weapon and she jerked it out of her purse without missing a beat.

He had to know she was closing in, but he didn't bother glancing back or taking a shot at her.

Her breath rushed in and out of her lungs as she pushed harder, fought for purchase in the ankle-deep snow. She couldn't risk stopping to take aim; she might lose him.

He hit the sidewalk on the next block. She emerged from the alley right on his heels.

She reached out…could almost grab his jacket…

A horn blared.

She jerked back, only then realizing she was in the middle of the street.

"You crazy, lady?" the driver shouted at her as he shook his fist out the window of his taxi.

"Damn." She shoved her right hand, the one with the gun, into her coat pocket, then surveyed the street. Pedestrians had stopped to stare.

The guy clad in black was gone.

She had stopped but he hadn't.

The horn blasted again and this time she did the fist-shaking. Anger pounded in her chest as she took one last look around before admitting defeat.

She'd lost him. She was definitely off her game.

When she'd rounded the corner of the next block, she tucked her weapon back into its special pocket inside her purse. This particular pocket was wrapped in a lightweight protective shield that prevented detection by security's X-ray machines and metal detectors.

A few blocks later and the UN Plaza came into view, flags proudly displayed for all to see. People, mostly employees at this hour, crowded through the entry doors. The line at the security checkpoint wasn't that long yet. Give it fifteen more minutes and there would be a row of impatient employees all the way out the door.

A latent print and retinal scan took hardly any time at all. Having her briefcase, purse and coat passed through the detection machines was a little more time-consuming. Once that was behind her, she made her way to the bank of elevators.

Her respiration had slowed back to normal as she boarded the elevator car with several exempt employees she recognized but whose names she didn't know. She interacted more with the ones who served their country in the same capacity as her.

She analyzed the few details she'd taken in about the man who'd been following her. Six feet or taller. One-hundred-and-eighty or one-hundred-and-ninety pounds, but it was hard to tell with the heavy coat. He'd worn all black, from the skull cap to the boots, but that wasn't uncommon in this city.

Who the hell would be following her? That this same man might have come into her apartment had her trying to remember the name of the last locksmith she'd used.

The elevator glided to a stop on the tenth floor. She would call the locksmith and then report the two incidents. Standard operating procedure. It didn't take a rocket scientist to know that whatever the hell was going on, it was job-related.

"Good morning, Miss Fox."

Sabrina produced a bright smile for Heather Bedford, the receptionist. "Good morning. Isn't the snow gorgeous?"

"Absolutely." The phone buzzed. "These are for you."

Sabrina accepted the three detailed notes Heather offered. It wasn't even nine yet, and people were already leaving messages. Sabrina thanked Heather and headed for her office.

Greetings were exchanged with several other colleagues before she reached her office door. Everyone wanted to talk about the snow and Christmas. The white stuff had generated a surge in holiday cheer. Only five more days until Christmas and she didn't even have a tree up in her apartment. Maybe she'd gotten lazy the past few years. She'd put up a tree the year before last…hadn't she? Drake had been there…

Okay, she wasn't about to blame her lack of interest in a tree again this year on him. He didn't deserve that much credit.

The thought had her angling for time to get the job done. Tonight, she decided. Tonight the tree and decorations would go up. Even if she had promised to go to her sister's for Christmas dinner, she could still enjoy the tree till then.

"Miss Fox!"

Sabrina looked up in time to see Geraldine Ramirez rushing toward her. "Good morning, Geraldine."

"Sorry to run you down like this, but Director Marx would like to see you ASAP."

"I'll drop my briefcase in my office and be right there," Sabrina assured her.

"I'll let him know."

Geraldine hustled off to inform her boss.

Sabrina glanced at her messages. Busy morning, and it had scarcely started. She needed to call that locksmith and write up the two incidents. She needed to think...to figure out just what was going on.

The idea that the call to Marx's office might have something to do with Ledger's visit cut through the rest of her thoughts.

A new deputy director. One from Interpol at that. The question as to how that would sit with the others intruded again. Not that Ledger wasn't a perfectly likeable guy, but he was an outsider. And why hadn't Marx warned them that something like this was coming down the pike?

She opened the door to her office and came face-to-face with Trainer and Big Hugh.

"We have to talk," Big Hugh deadpanned.

She moved inside and closed the door behind her. "Hey, guys, what's up?" She plopped her briefcase and purse onto her desk and shouldered out of her coat. "Talk fast. Marx is expecting me in his office like two minutes ago." She draped her coat on the tree in the corner.

"We heard a rumor that there's going to be a power shift." Trainer's gaze followed her movements as she fished her stiletto boots from her briefcase. "Have you heard anything about this?"

Sabrina toed off her snow boots one at a time. "Maybe that's what this morning's meeting is about." Telling them about Ledger's visit might be premature, especially in light of his reasons for coming to her.

"We heard through the grapevine," Big Hugh ventured, "that part of the new regime might include someone from Interpol." He pressed her with a knowing look. "Someone like Colin Ledger."

"Is he here?" Sabrina didn't see how they could be basing their assumptions on anything else. Ledger had to be here, his presence lending credence to the rumor they'd heard. Funny, she never heard the rumor.

Trainer nodded. "He's here."

"We want you to find out," Big Hugh explained. "Marx tells you everything."

Obviously not. Ledger's news last night had come as a shock to her.

"I'll see what I can do, boys." She smoothed the hem of her sweater. "Now, I gotta go."

"Be firm, Fox," Big Hugh encouraged as she moved toward the door. "Don't let Marx keep us in the dark."

"I'll do my best," she promised.

The floor had started to buzz with activity as Sabrina left her office. The elevators opened onto an elegant reception area and arriving personnel poured out. Two corridors—one going east, the other west—led to the various offices and were now congested with employees. Her office, along with those belonging to the team with whom she worked, were located on the west side of reception. The large clerical pool, mostly exempt employees as well as a few lower management officers, was housed on the east. Marx had a whole suite of offices down the hall and to the right of Sabrina's.

Once she passed through those double doors leading to the director's suite, she entered the private reception area where Geraldine's desk could be found.

Geraldine looked up long enough to say, "He's waiting for you, Miss Fox."

"Thank you."

Sabrina paused at the door and took a breath. If this was about Ledger…well, she wasn't sure she should be the one speaking for the team. Ledger was a great guy, but her feelings about him weren't completely objective.

Giving the door lever a downward twist, she pushed into the boss's office. "Good morning, Director Marx."

She was a little surprised that Ledger wasn't there. Maybe this wasn't about him after all.

"Fox. Excellent." Marx stood and gestured to one of the chairs flanking his desk. "We have a busy morning ahead of us."

That statement made her curious. "Do I have a

new assignment?" Usually he briefed the whole team when an assignment came up. She needed to tell him about finding her window open and then the guy who followed her this morning. The incidents could be a precursor to unforeseen trouble.

"We have a several things to talk about." He resumed his seat after she had taken hers. "Let's get the more imperative matters out of the way first."

Sabrina crossed her legs and gave him her undivided attention. She would take her cue from him.

"An opportunity has presented itself for us to get the jump on an ongoing operation that poses an international security risk. If we act quickly enough, we may be able to position ourselves in such a way to gain invaluable intelligence."

She didn't ask any questions at this point. No need. He would give her what he wanted her to know in his own way and time.

"There's a list of codes floating around Europe that we need to get our hands on, in a manner of speaking." He leaned back in his chair and tapped his fingers on the arms of his chair. "Unfortunately, we need it yesterday. These codes would allow our people access to a data flow that has previously been unavailable to us."

"I can leave today." These were the moments that kept her single and unfettered by husbands, children and dogs. This was why she'd made the decisions she had.

A slight nod acknowledged her readiness. Marx depended upon her more than he liked to admit. Very few females were willing to give up so much of life outside this business.

"Geraldine has made your travel arrangements already. You'll leave on an 11 a.m. flight." He picked up a red folder and passed it to her. "The courier has agreed to meet you in Paris. Once he has allowed you to make a digital copy of the codes, we'll wire the funds he requires into his account. He'll be able to verify the transfer by phone in a matter of seconds."

"The courier is Frederick Heilman?" Sabrina studied the man in the photograph. Brown hair, brown eyes, tall, relatively thin. No one she'd met before.

"Yes. You'll pose as a hooker, the two of you will have an encounter in the men's room. We don't want the courier compromised. If his contact has him under surveillance and suspects that the codes have been compromised, they'll be changed, which will defeat our purpose entirely."

"My travel cover?"

"You're supporting an American businessman, Ed Segelman. He's expecting a guide and trans-lator." Marx provided her with another file, this one manila in color. "Once you arrive in Paris, we'll provide a replacement at the pivotal time. You'll leave Segelman at the hotel and rendezvous with the courier tomorrow morning at 10 a.m. If all goes as planned, you'll be back on a flight to the U.S. by two. You'll be back within forty-eight hours. So no worries about this assignment interfering with your holiday plans."

A part of her wanted to say she wouldn't have minded one way or the other, but that would be counterproductive. She was supposed to be connecting more with her family, not seeking ways to avoid them.

"Not a problem, sir." She considered letting the other go for now, but that might be a mistake. "I have two incidents to report that may or may not be relevant to my status."

Concern filtered into his attentive expression.

"When I came home last night, someone had been in my apartment. Nothing was taken as far as I could tell, which is even more troubling."

"I'll have Hugh set up internal surveillance immediately. He'll need to conduct a sweep, as well."

She nodded. "Also, this morning, someone followed me to work. I wasn't able to make an ID." She didn't have to spell out the fact that she'd lost him.

"This is troubling." Marx seemed to consider the information a moment. "Your assignment is top priority, so we'll move forward with that.

Meanwhile, I'll have Hugh and Trainer look into these incidents. An old enemy may have tracked you down. We'll handle the situation."

"Thank you, sir." She stood. She should have told him about the calls…but she didn't. "I'll make preparations for the assignment."

Marx held up a hand for her to hold on a moment. "There's something else we need to talk about, Fox. I'll only take a moment more of your time."

Oh, damn, here it came. She lowered back into her chair. "Of course."

"I understand Ledger spoke to you last night."

To say that she was startled would be a huge understatement. "Yes, he did." That meant Marx was privy to how Ledger felt about her. Dammit, she should never have shared that kiss with him. She'd expected the Ledger talk to come from a different perspective.

"I need to make sure you understand why this change is considered necessary to IT&PA."

"I assume as the demands on our organization increase that there's need for additional oversight." She assumed a lot of other things, but she wasn't about to mention her fear that Marx might be considering retirement. He was swiftly approaching sixty. She hoped like hell that wasn't the case. Then there was the merger option of IT&PA and Interpol she'd heard rumors of. Again, her thoughts were more speculation than anything else.

Marx took a long, deep breath and then let it out slowly, wearily. A frown started to nag at her forehead. She'd never known him to sound so tired. Maybe the load was getting to him. Maybe that was the reason for bringing in a deputy after years of successful operation without one.

"This was always the plan, Fox. An American would run IT&PA for four or five years, and then one of our fine counterparts from across the pond would have a turn. It was the best way to ensure the two organizations blended fully, that intelligence sharing was optimal."

As surprised as she was by the revelation, it made sense. That sort of deal would ensure everyone was on the same page. No hidden agendas. No secrets.

"The transition was supposed to have occurred two years ago, but there was a complication."

Another revelation quaked through her, this one with an entirely different impact.

He was talking about Drake and his abrupt departure from Interpol. He didn't have to say so; she knew it in her gut.

"We've had a bit of back and forth since," Marx continued, "and here we are. It is their turn and they're not going to wait any longer. I suppose I can't blame Interpol. It was the deal we made. Things didn't work out two years ago but now they're ready to assume the helm."

Marx sighed. "Considering Ledger's outstanding reputation, I'm certain he'll do a fine job. My only concern is with the initial unrest here."

He flared his hands as if he weren't sure about this next part. "We should have had this talk long ago, but after what happened with Drake, I wasn't so sure what would happen. I knew this was coming."

Sabrina worked hard to keep the Drake part out of her head just then. She could analyze that later. Right now, she needed to focus. "So, Ledger will take over right away?"

"Basically. Making him deputy now will, hopefully, prevent some of the hard feelings various people might have once he rises to the position of director in a few months and I retire. We want this transition to go as smoothly as possible."

"So." She cleared her throat. The fact that Marx would retire kept echoing in her brain. "It's a done deal with Ledger?"

Marx made one of those gestures with his hands that indicated it was anybody's guess. "He has until the day after Christmas to make his final decision. If he turns down the position, which I don't anticipate he'll do, then we're back to square one. Interpol will have to regroup and come up with another candidate. You see my dilemma?"

Definitely. How did a director brief his people when he wasn't sure what was going to happen? She let go of the breath she'd been holding. At least he didn't seem to know that Ledger was holding out because of her.

"I appreciate you giving me notice on how this may play out."

"I don't want you worrying about this transition now, Fox. I need you to get me those codes."

She nodded. "I won't fail, sir." She never had before...except that once and that hadn't been her fault, nor was it even a failure. The ultimate goal had been achieved, just not by her. She stood, feeling a little light-headed. "I'll get going now."

She'd almost made it to the door, was still reeling just a little from all she'd learned, when Marx waylaid her once more.

"Just one more thing, Fox."

"Yes, sir?"

"I'd like to keep this quiet for now. There will be an official announcement after Christmas. I know you and your team are close, but I need to ensure the change is actually going to go through this time before we put everyone in emotional turmoil."

She nodded. "I understand."

"Do one more thing for me, Fox."

"Sir?"

"Take special care on this one. I've kind of grown attached to you. I'd like to believe you'll still be here keeping an eye on Ledger after I'm gone. You never know about those Brits."

A smile prodded its way past her troubling thoughts. "Damn straight I'll be here, sir. I won't cut him a millimeter of slack."

"That's what I'm counting on."

This time he let her go. She walked straight through Geraldine's office without stopping. Her flight left in two and a half hours. That was a plenty good enough reason not to talk to anyone.

"Agent Fox."

She stalled in the corridor outside her office. She'd almost made it.

That Ledger was the one to interrupt her escape only made bad matters worse.

"I don't have time to talk right now." She manufactured a smile for him. "I have a flight in just over two hours." She reached for her door, hoped he would leave it at that.

His hand settled gently on her arm. "Sabrina, I know this is difficult. Marx is a grand chap and I know you're very attached to him, but this is how the powers that be want things. Both he and I are merely playing by the rules imposed from above."

She shifted so that she could look him directly in the eye. "I understand, but I am in a hurry. So maybe we can talk when I get back." He'd likely been brought up to speed on all ongoing missions, including hers.

Those long, strong fingers squeezed her arm. "Don't forget to consider my offer."

He wasn't going to make this easy. "Sure thing."

She couldn't think about any of this right now.

The mission was what mattered.

As long as she got that done, she could deal with the rest later.

She was Sabrina Fox, a kick-butt secret agent.

Marx had been telling her that for years; she wasn't about to prove him wrong now.

CHAPTER SEVEN

"WHAT WE HAVE here is your typical long-weekend-in-Paris ensemble."

Sabrina paid close attention as Angie provided the details of the wardrobe and accessories currently littered across her desk for today's unexpected mission. Thank God for Angie. She could put together a wardrobe for any place, any time of year, in mere minutes.

"I checked the five-day forecast and the weather conditions are running about the same as here, with a little less of the white stuff."

She directed Sabrina's attention to the miniskirt and tight, scoop necked sweater for her rendezvous with the courier. Sabrina nodded. She'd definitely be showcasing some cleavage with that outfit. Since her cover for meeting the courier was as a hooker, a miniskirt and lots of cleavage were indispensable.

"Looks good, Angie." Sabrina gave her an appreciative pat on the shoulder. "I can't think of a thing you've forgotten." Cosmetics and other necessities had been packed separately in a small bag that would fit easily into the one suitcase Sabrina would carry.

"I've set aside your travel wear." She indicated the black slacks and sweater draped across the chair in front of Sabrina's desk. "I'd suggest the boots with the lower heel for the trip."

"Sounds good." Sabrina sat those boots aside.

"So, let's pack," Angie suggested.

Together they quickly assembled the mini-wardrobe and the cosmetic bag into the twenty-six-inch expandable upright. Just enough room. That was another thing Angie could do with a single glance, determine the correct size of suitcase required. It was uncanny.

"Knock, knock."

"Come in," Sabrina called over her shoulder.

Big Hugh opened the door into Sabrina's office a little wider and poked his head in. "Are you ladies ready for me and my goodies?"

"Always." Sabrina zipped the suitcase. Whatever Big Hugh had for her would go into her shoulder bag.

He stepped into her office and closed the door firmly behind him. His portion of the mission prep would require complete privacy.

"I have a number of gadgets for you." Big Hugh did love the gadgets. He was the first to try them out whenever research delivered a new shipment of cutting-edge technology. He was like a kid with all of FAO Schwarz to explore after closing time.

"The digital camera." Sabrina spotted it immediately. A beautiful tube of lipstick with jeweled embellishments. A gorgeous piece, gadgetry aside.

"Magnificent, isn't it?" Hugh beamed as if he'd designed the piece himself.

"Truly." She studied the tube from all angles. No way anyone would ever guess its actual purpose.

"It's even your favorite shade."

Now that was amazing. She opened it and sure enough, there it was, Very Sexy Red.

"What's next?" The stuff those research guys came up with was mind-boggling.

"Ink pen." He clicked the top, causing the writing tip to appear. "One poke with this and your enemy won't be getting up for a while. Not deadly, but extremely potent and lightning fast. Puts an average-size man down for at least sixty minutes."

She decided to tuck the pen into the small zipper compartment inside the shoulder bag. Using it to sign a receipt definitely would not be a good idea. Fishing around inside her purse and accidentally poking herself wouldn't be, either.

"The coup de grâce." Hugh presented her with a typical-looking hairbrush. "When you grasp the handle—" he picked up the brush "—just apply a little extra pressure and voilà!" A six-inch blade sprang forth.

"The blade won't show up on the X-ray when I send my bag through security?"

He shook his head. "There's a protective coating on the steel. It's virtually undetectable." He pressed the tip of the blade against her brass name plate and forced it back into the brush. "Brand-new technology."

"Cool." She gave the brush a once-over and then slipped it into her bag. "What about other weapons?" While he brought her up to speed on what would be available, she transferred her wallet and other essential items from her purse to the shoulder bag she would use for the trip.

"Firepower will be waiting for you at the hotel desk. Our contact in Paris has taken care of our request. One 9mm Glock with the standard hair trigger and a dainty .22 for better concealment."

"Very good."

Trainer barged into Sabrina's office. "Why wasn't I invited to this party?" He closed the door behind him and pointed an annoyed face at Sabrina. "I am a part of this team, am I not?"

"I knew you wouldn't want to see the panties I selected for Agent Fox," Angie said with a smirk. "We all know how you feel about sexual harassment. We felt it was our obligation to protect you from the moment."

Trainer peeked over at the black suitcase. "I can't believe I missed that. What color? More pink?" He surveyed Angie as if he wondered what she might be wearing. "Red, maybe?"

"Get out of here, Trainer," Angie groused. "You are too nasty."

Trainer leaned closer to her. "Perhaps you don't know this, Ang, but in some circles nasty is actually considered incredibly sexy."

The stoutly built woman threw up her hands. "I'm out of here. There's way too much testosterone in this room now."

"Thanks, Angie." Sabrina followed up the remark with an appreciative smile.

"Have a safe trip, Fox. Get back here for Christmas." She winked at Sabrina. "Don't go spending the holiday with some sexy Frenchman."

As soon as the door closed behind Angie, Big Hugh and Trainer rounded on Sabrina.

"Okay, what gives?" Trainer demanded. "Why is Ledger hanging around?"

"Did Marx tell you anything?" Big Hugh wanted to know. "Is Ledger trying to horn in on us?"

Sabrina didn't want to think about Ledger or his ultimatum. Now that she knew the director's motive for the abrupt move in making him deputy,

Ledger's visit last night felt exactly like an ultimatum. He had known Marx would brief her on the situation. He'd put the decision in her hands. Tell him to get lost or give up her position. That was the bottom line. If they pursued a relationship, her career at IT&PA would be over since he would be her boss.

Maintaining the status quo of their professional relationship would be a slap in her new boss's face. Not a good way to start off that working relationship. That he'd put her in this position made her mad as hell. If he thought for one second that he could push her into a relationship, he was dead wrong. Not that he'd actually been pushy, but he'd definitely been persistent.

"Come on, what did Marx tell you?" Big Hugh prodded, dragging her from her troubling thoughts. "Besides the details of the mission, I mean."

"He…ah…"

She hated doing this, but Marx had asked her to keep the change in command quiet for now. He would be *retiring.* She could scarcely believe it, and she'd heard it with her own ears, straight from his mouth.

"He mentioned that he and Ledger were working on executive issues. In fact," she said in hopes of satisfying her curious colleagues with a meager bone, "Ledger is probably with him right now hashing out those very issues."

Big Hugh shook his head. "Executive issues, you say? What the hell does that mean?"

Sabrina nodded as she gathered her travel wear. She should get changed and head to the airport. "That's what he said. Who knows what it means?"

"Sounds like trouble," Trainer commented. "Ledger could be transferring here as a permanent Interpol counterpart. I'm not sure how I feel about that. He likes stealing the show."

Trainer definitely wasn't the only one who thought that about Ledger, but Sabrina had to keep her feelings to herself.

"Gotta get dressed, boys. Let me know if you hear any interesting rumors."

When the two had wandered out of her office, both still speculating as to what Ledger was up to, she locked the door and prepared for the trip.

She hadn't noticed the coat until she reached for her own on the tree in the corner. Leather, thigh-length, with a plush animal print lining for warmth. A pair of black, fur-lined gloves was stuffed in the pockets. Angie covered every last detail.

With a final perusal of her office, she remembered to grab an extra, fully charged battery for her cell phone. She might not have the time or the opportunity to do any charging the usual way.

As she headed for the elevator with her suitcase and new shoulder bag, she glanced toward the suite of offices belonging to Director Marx.

He was retiring.

It seemed impossible. He defined IT&PA.

How would life without him be like here?

She didn't want to think about that right now. In fact she didn't want to think about any of it at all. But at some point she would have to.

Until then, she pushed the confusing idea away.

Sabrina said goodbye to the receptionist and punched the call button for the elevator.

Dwelling on the news Marx had conveyed or the other strange stuff going on in her life would be detrimental to this mission. The last thing he'd asked of her was to be sure she came back alive. To do that, she had to stay focused.

No matter what other surprises life had in store for her just now, staying alive was paramount to knowing how this all ended.

THE HOTEL NAPOLÉON of Paris was located next to the Arc de Triomphe and the famous Avenue des Champs-Élysées and the Lido. The Eiffel Tower could be seen from the windows of the deluxe rooms and better suites, and the Louvre, the Opera House and the Congress & Exhibition Center were mere steps away. A luxury art deco building with all the modern conveniences any widely traveled American would expect in a five-star hotel. Not shabby at all.

The lobby beyond the glass front entrance

boasted gleaming marble floors and a richly
finished, ornate wood reception desk. Red velvet
chairs, lush drapes and glittering chandeliers com-
pleted the affluent atmosphere. Royal blue carpet
lined the stairs, and brass accessories provided
the perfect finishing touch. Fine living at its best.

Arriving in the middle of the night had its
perks. The lobby was deserted save for hotel employees.

Ed Segelman, the American businessman with
whom she was scheduled to have breakfast in a
few hours, had divine taste. Unfortunately, she
and Mr. Segelman would never meet. The final
bottle of water he'd accepted on his flight had
been laced with a mild designer bug to keep him
under the weather for approximately twenty-four
hours. Whether Sabrina was back at the hotel
within that time or not, another IT&PA employee
would step in to assist Mr. Segelman with his
business in Paris.

Since Sabrina had not stayed in this particular
hotel during any of her previous trips to Paris, she
hoped the beds were as comfortable as the lavish
decor was pleasing to the discerning eye.

Sabrina accepted the key from the clerk. Since
he didn't mention a package, she decided to ask
if he had one for her.

He rummaged around behind the desk until he
found what he was looking for. Instead of handing

the package to her, he passed it to the bellhop, who hovered nearby in anticipation of seeing her to her room.

Sabrina didn't argue. Let the bellhop carry her suitcase and package. It was late, or early depending upon the way one looked at it. She just wanted to crawl into bed and go to sleep. After she'd inspected her weapons, of course.

Fifth floor. Room 568. Third room on the left beyond the elevator. She was impressed all over again with her accommodations.

After tipping the bellhop, she was finally alone in her room. She stripped off her clothes and climbed beneath the covers, naked save for her black panties and bra. She didn't care that the drapes were open to the magnificent view beyond the window, including the Eiffel Tower. It was 2 a.m. She needed sleep now. Besides, no one in Paris would care if she cavorted in front of an open window while wearing nothing at all.

Before surrendering to her body's exhaustion, she forced herself to open the box and examine the 9mm and the .22. The thigh holster for the .22 was something new and rather intriguing, but not so much so to keep her from giving in to sleep.

She was too tired to make her brain or her eyes work at this point.

As she drifted toward sleep she considered that she should have called Leslie to let her know she

was leaving the country. If Sabrina were hospital-
ized or killed while she was in Paris her sister
would hold the fact that she hadn't kept her
informed against her.

Too bad.

But part of this new bonding thing included
considering her sister's feelings. The least she
could do was let her know when she left the
country.

Maybe she'd call tomorrow if there was time.

Assuming all went as planned.

SOMETHING HAD GONE terribly wrong.

Sabrina had just stepped out of the shower
when her room phone clattered noisily.

Ed Segelman was waiting for her in the restaurant dining room. He didn't mind waiting, he
assured her. He would order for both of them.

He wasn't supposed to be able to get out of bed
at this point. What the hell had gone wrong?

She was supposed to meet the courier at the
train station at ten. The outfit for going to the train
station wasn't exactly the usual office wear. But
there wouldn't be time to change. Oh well, maybe
the skirt would gain her some points with
Segelman. At least enough to make up for
showing up late at their breakfast meeting.

A quick phone call to Big Hugh, despite the fact
that it was the middle of the night in New York,

had confirmed her suspicions. The drug in the laced water would kick in eventually, unless someone failed to do their part. In which case, she was screwed.

If the bug didn't take effect during the next thirty minutes she would have a hell of a time making the train station on time.

With her black leather mini, black low neck sweater and boots, she looked ready for a night out on the town rather than a business meeting. She carried her leather coat and the red scarf. The courier would be looking for the red scarf.

The restaurant was every bit as elegant as the hotel. As promised, Segelman waited patiently at a table for two near the wall of windows that looked out over the Champs-Élysées.

Ed Segelman was an attractive man nearing fifty. He wore a gray suit and shirt with a jazzy purple tie to set it off. He had a terrific personality and didn't seem put off by the fact that she was late or by her suspect attire. He appeared to go with the flow extremely well. Not at all like most high-strung executives.

He told her all about his personalized shipping business and she reminded herself to look impressed. She'd read his bio. The man had invented a number of software packages for state-of-the-art tracking systems. If all went as planned, his company would merge with a French company that would allow for cornering the market between the U.S. and Europe.

"I have a revised agenda for the next two days," Segelman told her as his right hand dived into his briefcase. "Meetings have a way of getting bumped up or delayed with these Frenchmen."

Sabrina smiled while suppressing a trickle of panic. She had to ditch this guy ASAP. First, she needed a backup plan. Maybe the guy was immune to the bug they'd given him. Whatever the hell was wrong, she didn't have time for this problem, but making IT&PA look bad carried risks of its own. A stellar reputation was essential to maintaining that all-important cover.

Keeping her panic to a minimum, she accepted the revised agenda. "Thank you."

Pretending to review the document, she'd almost decided that using the ink pen Hugh had provided would be necessary when Segelman abruptly paled.

"Oh, my." He stood and rushed from the table.

Sabrina visually tracked his escape to the men's room. About time.

Better late than never, she supposed as she nibbled at the fruit plate the waiter delivered. Might as well eat. The food on the plane had pretty much sucked.

Five minutes passed and Segelman still hadn't returned.

After ten minutes, she decided that checking on him was necessary. He was only supposed to get sick, not die. She'd already lost far too much time, but she couldn't exactly get up and walk out without ensuring he made it back to his room.

The waiter who had served their table caught her halfway across the dining room.

"Madame, I am afraid Monsieur Segelman has taken ill. He has returned to his room."

"Merci."

Sabrina took the elevator to the sixth floor and located Segelman's room. She knocked twice before she heard a feeble response.

"Mr. Segelman, this is Sabrina," she called through the door. "Are you all right, sir?"

The door opened. She stepped inside the room just in time to see Segelman fall across the bed.

"I don't know what the problem is, but I know I can't leave this room."

She could imagine the reasons why.

"Is there anything I can do, sir? Anyone I should call?"

"No…I'll cancel today's meetings. Check in with me later this afternoon about the changes in our agenda. I'm sure I'll be fine by then."

"Yes, sir."

He waved her off when she made no move to leave. "Go. Enjoy your day in Paris."

"I'll see you this afternoon, then."

Sabrina was out the door and down the hall as fast as she could move without breaking into a dead run. She would be cutting it damn close.

Zooming across the lobby, she exited the front entrance of the hotel and was relieved to see a taxi parked at the curb. She darted past several arriving guests and grabbed the door before anyone else could get close. All those years in Manhattan had been perfect training for snagging a cab.

"Gare de l'Est, rapidement!"

The driver acknowledged the destination with a nod and sped away from the curb. As long as they didn't encounter any traffic problems she should be on schedule.

The hiccup in Segelman's reaction to the nasty little bug had set the tone for the whole day. Tense. She didn't like tense. All it would take was one delay to close this window of opportunity.

She couldn't let that happen. She'd tasted the bitter taint of failure once. Once was enough.

CHAPTER EIGHT

THE DRIVER WHIZZED ALONG the roundabout circling the Arc de Triomphe. Sabrina chose not to watch as he merged into the controlled chaos of other vehicles rotating counterclockwise. Weaving and dodging, the taxi would eventually spiral back out of the flow of traffic with the same lethal ease with which he'd merged. Far too horrifying a maneuver to watch.

She directed her attention to the famous sights of Charles de Gaulle-Étoile. The Eiffel Tower, the Champs Élysées, and the Place de la Concorde. No matter that she'd seen them all dozens of times, there was something about Paris that made her want to admire the architecture over and over again.

After bearing right, the driver zipped along the boulevard, tires bumping over cobblestones, allowing Sabrina to take a deep breath once more.

French drivers were far more inclined to make dicey maneuvers than even New York drivers. And that was saying something.

On the way to her destination, Sabrina visualized her contact, the courier. She checked the digital camera disguised as a lipstick and the .22 tucked into her boot. The tight miniskirt had preempted any possibility of wearing the thigh holster. The 9mm was in her shoulder bag, along with the pen, brush, her passport, Euros and a credit card.

She checked the time on her cell phone: 9:40. Though she was definitely cutting it close, she would make it. The farther they moved from the center of the city, the less likely they were to encounter any unavoidable traffic gridlock.

The Christmas decorations reminded her that there were only four days left. If for any reason she didn't make it back to the States in time, she had a feeling her mother and sister would be far more disappointed this time. She'd have to make sure that didn't happen.

And if she did make it back and they found out she'd been in Paris just before Christmas without doing any gift shopping, her name would really be mud. No one else in her family had ever traveled outside the U.S.

No problem. Once she had the digital copies of the codes, she would head back to Paris, pop into one of her favorite shops, en route to the airport of course, and grab a few gift items.

No sweat.

A few minutes later, the Gare de l'Est station came into view with its stately columns and statues. Like the rest of Paris, centuries of history had taken place in the square around the station that dated back two centuries or more.

"*Merci.*" Sabrina paid the fare before emerging from the vehicle, then hurried across the cobble-stoned square and through the access arcade with its grand paintings and sculptures. Under normal circumstances, she would have loved to linger and admire the work of each artist, but there was no time to indulge the tourist in her. She was cutting it way too close for comfort.

She checked the overhead signs for the platform she needed and then took the appropriate escalator. One of Paris's main stations, Gare de l'Est had its share of commuters rushing to catch their trains. Thousands of people, local and tourists alike, passed through each day.

Scanning the faces for her contact, she moved with the flow of commuters until she reached the designated platform.

Sabrina adjusted her scarf. Three minutes to ten. After selecting the best scouting position, she slipped into character by eying every male that crossed her path. She adopted a provocative stance and smiled in blatant invitation.

Most of the men who passed noticed her, which made her search somewhat easier. She reviewed what she knew about her contact—brown hair, brown eyes, six-one, one hundred and sixty pounds. Approximately thirty-years-old and probably of German descent. His name was Frederick Heilman. At least that was the one he went by, an alias no doubt.

At precisely 10 a.m. a train roared up to the platform. The doors opened and the mass exodus commenced. She grew more alert as the crowd thickened and then thinned with the boarding of passengers and the rush toward the escalators of those disembarking. She craned her neck this way and that in attempt to scan each passenger, coming or going.

The courier, Heilman, was supposed to look for her but she didn't trust anyone except her team in matters such as this. Couriers were human, after all, subject to fear, panic, and, most commonly, greed. She intensified her vigilance, carefully screening every face from her vantage point.

Then she saw him.

He saw her, as well.

Their gazes locked, and seconds later recognition registered on his face. No way to miss it, not even from a good ten yards.

For a few tense seconds more, he just stood there, staring at her. She refrained from making the first move, he was supposed to approach her.

As if fate had rolled out of bed this morning and

decided to ruin her day, her contact did exactly what he wasn't supposed to.

He boarded the train.

She had no choice but to follow him.

She boarded at the nearest door. The train would pull away from the platform any second. Failing to be on with the courier would be a major mistake.

Now all she had to do was find him.

She weaved her way through the open passenger cars, scanning the packed crowd. As she did, she considered why he would have boarded this particular train rather than coming over to talk to her as planned. There had to have been a new development she didn't know about.

Had he been followed?

Was this move about protecting the codes?

Or had he decided that he didn't dare double-cross his employer? And there was always the chance he'd sold out to a higher bidder.

The only way to know was to locate him and to keep him under surveillance until an opportunity to confront him presented itself. As long as he didn't get off this train without her knowing it, finding him wouldn't be that complicated.

As the train began to roll away from the platform final frantic attempts to find seats made moving forward more difficult. Sabrina kept her eyes peeled and struggled with her growing impatience. Long minutes later, she'd explored every passenger car.

The cars comprised of compartments proved a lot less congested. But they also presented a problem of their own: the only way to find out who was inside the small rooms was to knock and get herself invited inside, or just open the door and look.

In deference to the time, she opted for the latter. Most of the passengers were still settling in, which meant they hadn't gotten around to securing doors. Pretending she was lost or had selected the wrong compartment was a completely acceptable excuse.

She'd reached the fourth compartment in the second car when she found him.

Barging in as she had at all the other rooms, she came face-to-face with the business end of a .40 calibre Ruger. Her heart rate accelerated. At least she'd found him. And now she had her answer— he'd sold out to someone else.

"Close the door."

Yep, German. Though the words were English, the accent was unmistakable.

Going a step farther than he asked, she closed the door and locked it.

"What's going on, Heilman? We had a deal."

"That was before your people tried to kill me as I left my hotel this morning."

Now there was an original twist. "I don't know

what you're talking about, Heilman. You've apparently been misinformed. If someone tried to kill you, it wasn't my people."

"Don't lie to me." His hand, the one with the Ruger pointed at her head, shook.

Despite the fact that it was December and cold as hell, a line of sweat had broken out on his brow. Not a good sign for either of them.

"Why would I lie to you?" she asked matter-of-factly. "You have a gun pointed at my head. It's only four days until Christmas. I'm not interested in dying this week."

"I can't take the risk." The hysteria in his eyes signaled that this wasn't him getting cold feet or having second thoughts. This guy was on the edge. Unfortunately, she was poised on that slippery precipice right alongside him without a rope or parachute.

"Let's both just take a breath," she suggested, careful to keep her hands in full view and her voice as calm as possible. He was scared. Fear blocked reason. If she could get him to reason out the situation, he'd see that she wouldn't be here if her people had tried to kill him.

"Why should I listen to anything you have to say when you'll probably shoot me as soon as you have what you want? Isn't that the plan?"

Somebody really had gotten to him.

"Sorry, Heilman, but that's not the plan at all.

In fact, it's extremely important to me that you complete your mission once I've copied the codes. Think about it. Killing you would defeat my purpose entirely. The codes are useless if you don't complete your mission."

He blinked, seemed to consider her words. Any minute now, the train would start to pick up speed as it rolled away from the station. Settling this issue quickly was imperative. The longer they haggled, the more likely they were to be seen together by someone watching for this very scenario.

Heilman blew out a heavy breath. "We have a problem, I'm afraid."

"What kind of problem?" She braced for the worst news.

"I was worried so I sent the codes with a different courier."

Now there was some seriously bad news.

"Talk to me, Heilman. I need those codes." Dammit. The other courier could be anyone, anywhere. Her tension sharpened. "I need the ID of the other courier and his destination."

He lowered his weapon as if he'd suddenly grown too weary to hold it up. "I don't know which route he took, but he—"

The sharp crack of breaking glass sounded behind him.

His eyes rounded and his lips continued to move but the words were silent.

He fell forward and slumped into her arms.

His weight dragged Sabrina down to her knees.

Her gaze moved from the hole in the back of his parka to the shattered glass of the train window. The shot had come from somewhere on the platform. If the enemy knew they were on this train, there would be someone on board to take care of any final loose ends. Nothing would be left to chance.

Just to be sure he hadn't lied to her, she quickly rolled the dead man onto his back and checked him for the codes. The briefcase he carried was empty. So were his pockets and any other place he might hide what she needed.

Grunting with the effort, she hefted his dead weight onto the seat into a sitting position and arranged him as if he were sleeping. She placed his briefcase on the seat next to him.

Before she could consider leaving the compart-ment, she needed to make a few changes. She removed the flashy red scarf. She shoved it beneath the seat that converted for sleeping. Shedding her coat, she turned it inside out so that the animal print lining showed before pulling it back on.

She needed to get out of this compartment and to the lounge car where she could mingle with the crowd until they reached the next stop. Going back to one of the passenger cars would make her a sitting duck. Other than jumping out the window, there was no escape. The lounge car would provide far more opportunities for blending in.

The only question now was, would the enemy be waiting outside this door for her?

Only one way to find out.

Sabrina flattened against the wall next to the door, then reached for the latch to open it. She allowed the door to swing inward and steeled herself for any abrupt moves.

No movement, no sound other than the steady whir and hum of the train rushing along its track.

She edged into the corridor outside the compartment. Clear left. Clear right.

Left would take her in the direction of the lounge car. Keeping a watch on the corridor behind her, she moved forward. As soon as she was in an optimal position for protecting herself, she would put a call in to Big Hugh. They had been double-crossed. She also needed to know if he'd picked up any intelligence indicating who the new courier might be or the final destination.

If she couldn't locate the new courier, she would have to try and intercept the codes before they reached their final destination. The latter would make for a considerably riskier save, but the codes were essential to national security. NSA needed them in order to access intelligence previously off limits. That was all she needed to know.

No matter how high any agent's clearance was, all intelligence was still doled out on a need-to-know basis.

Upon reaching the lounge car, Sabrina took a moment to study the crowd. The bar was backed up with patrons needing something more than coffee, even at this early hour. Those who'd arrived early were already stationed at the well-dressed tables scattered along the length of the car. Bone china and polished silver decorated each place setting atop the pristine white linen. A small crystal vase adorned with a single flower served as centerpieces. Ashtrays had already started to overflow, and cigarette smoke hung in the air.

The flashes of brazen male approval tossed her way allowed her to discount as a no threat most men she encountered. To think for even a second that she'd get lucky and the bad guys had all stayed behind at Gare de l'Est would be a mistake. If the enemy knew about her, and obviously they did, great measures would be taken to see that any further security risk she represented was neutralized. Her adversary would know that she would proceed with countermeasures.

Two men stood, gathered their coats, and left their table near the far end of the lounge car. Sabrina moved quickly in that direction and claimed a seat with her back to the wall and a full view of the entire car, including the exit to the dining car.

The waiter breezed by. "You wish to order, madame?"

"Wine, please." Sabrina shifted her attention to the waiter just long enough to provide the perfunctory smile.

The waiter nodded and continued on toward the double doors that led into the adjoining kitchen. Sabrina surveyed the faces of those seated around her, as well as the faces of the waiters. The ability to weave through crowded tables while carrying a loaded tray with the train rushing along the track at speeds of more than one hundred miles per hour never ceased to amaze her.

She reached into her bag and withdrew her phone. Updating Protocol while she had the opportunity would be a smart move. Once the number was entered, a single ring echoed across the line and then the automated voice. She then entered her numerical code and stated her code phrase for voice analysis.

Seconds later that same automated voice asked, "Status?"

"Initiating Plan B." The statement provided Protocol with the status of her mission: rendezvous unsuccessful. Providing her position would not be necessary since the GPS in her phone would transmit that information. Based on her position, a new destination would be triangulated. Upon her arrival at the new destination, she would pick up new orders.

No matter how secure the line, orders were never transmitted via phone. The brief delay on the other end of the line let her know that her next move was being verified.

"Troyes is your destination."

Sabrina severed the connection and dropped her phone back into her bag.

Troyes was a ninety-minute train ride from Paris. She didn't have to ask if this particular train was headed that way. The destination would not have been selected otherwise.

The waiter arrived with her wine. She paid the tab and considered for the first time that she didn't actually have a ticket to cover the fare. She would need to purchase one and pay the necessary supplement.

Each new face that entered the car was quickly scrutinized. Posture and movement were assessed for threat. So far she saw no reason to elevate her alert status.

The waiter approached her table. Too soon to refresh her drink.

"Madame, this is for you." He placed a folded piece of paper on her table.

When he would have moved away, she asked, "Do I have a secret admirer?"

The waiter smiled. "Apparently so, madame. He asked that I deliver the note to the blond beauty wearing the sexy skirt."

"*Merci.*"

Sabrina checked the crowd again. She saw no one she recognized. No one who appeared to be watching her. She opened the note and glanced at the words scrawled there in bold, broad strokes.

I'm waiting.

The car and compartment number was listed but they scarcely registered. Her brain kept denying what her heart knew. Her pulse rate accelerated.

Drake's handwriting.

She would recognize his bold flair anywhere.

Her gaze moved over the patrons, searching for the face she'd sworn she never wanted to see again as long as she lived.

It was possible the note was a forgery. It wasn't totally out of the realm of possibility that an elaborate scheme had been put into place in order to see that she didn't make it off this train.

Most anything was possible.

But every instinct screamed at her that this was the real thing.

Eric Drake…the Dragon…was on this train.

CHAPTER NINE

THE HYPNOTIC DRONE of the train was the only sound that accompanied her to her destination. The corridor was clear in both directions, the compartments fairly quiet beyond their closed doors. The soft hum of music drifted from one, a hushed conversation from another, while the dialogue from a movie seeped beyond the enclosing walls of yet another.

The .22 rested in her palm, her coat draped over her arm to camouflage the weapon.

She reached the compartment she sought, pressed against the wall next to the door and listened.

Silence radiated beyond the closed door. She steeled herself, then reached up with her left hand to knock on the door.

"Don't do that."

She pivoted to face the low voice she would have recognized in a hurricane.

Eric Drake.

Her pulse hit full throttle before the idea that

the man towering over her was, in fact, Eric Drake
had even penetrated her brain.

Coal-black hair, piercing blue eyes.

Still as handsome as sin itself. And every bit as
lethal.

"This way." He jerked his head toward the compartment behind him. The one in which he'd been
waiting, it seemed.

Fury lashed through her. She pulled the coat
back from her right hand just far enough for him
to see the muzzle of the .22. "I don't think so."

He shrugged and then stepped back inside the
open door of the compartment. "Suit yourself,
Fox. But just so you know," he went on smugly,
"they're searching the train for you at this very
moment. Standing around out here in the open
isn't exactly a brilliant move."

Her first impulse was to shoot him.

But then she'd just have to deal with the hassle
of the French police.

He wasn't worth the trouble.

She glanced left and then right before crossing
the threshold into enemy territory.

"What the hell do you want, Drake?" Her voice
didn't reflect anywhere near the full extent of her
white-hot rage, but it came close.

He reached past her—she flinched—and
shoved the door shut. "We should probably lock

that door," he suggested in that cavalier tone that made her want to kick the hell out of him.

She stepped aside, her weapon still trained on him, center chest, and let him secure the door just in case he wasn't lying.

"What do you want, Drake?"

That nothing about him had changed in two years infuriated her all the more. Still as strong and virile as ever. The beat-up leather bomber jacket, Harvard sweater and worn soft jeans were classic Drake. He loved looking like your typical American tourist, all the way down to the Nike sneakers. But that voice...that clever Welsh accent was unmistakable.

"You've been targeted for elimination." Those blue eyes settled heavily on hers. "I'm here to make sure that doesn't happen."

If he'd said Santa wanted to see her at the North Pole she wouldn't have been more stunned. What kind of fool did he take her for?

"Yeah," she scoffed, "right. Now what is it you really want?"

He pursed those full, firm lips and tsk-tsked annoyingly. "You never used to be this cynical, Sabrina. Perhaps you need a vacation. Please tell me you're not still working too hard."

The blow would have carried more weight if she'd used her right hand but since the .22 was in the way, she went with her left. She slapped him as hard as she could. That he scarcely winced gave her no satisfaction whatsoever. He had no right to wonder what she did anymore. He'd lost that right when he cheated on her.

"I'm calling you in, Drake. You know the penalty for interfering with a mission. Your friends at Interpol won't be happy. Even ex-agents have to follow the rules." She shook off the ache in her left hand and jammed it into her bag in search of her phone. Whatever he was up to, he wasn't going to get in her way.

"If you let Interpol know I'm here, we'll both end up dead."

"What?" This had to be a trick. "Why would anyone want to eliminate you? You're out of the business."

"I didn't simply resign two years ago."

Two years ago, they'd worked that joint mission. He'd screwed her over and walked away. He'd betrayed her in the worst way. She shoved those thoughts out of her head. She would not let her mind wander down that damned road.

She held up her hands, refused to feel or think anything where he was concerned. "You know what? I don't give a damn what's going on with you, now or then. I'm out of here." She could make the call someplace else, anywhere but here.

He snagged her by the arm. "Not so fast."

Jerking free of his hold, she waved the .22. "I don't have time for this, whatever the hell this is.

Now, back off." She hated that her emotions were boiling so close to the surface. Absolutely hated that he could make her feel this way.

"I can't let you go back out there, Sabrina." He reached for her again, but she gave him a look that said, "touch me and you're dead," so he backed off. "Let's just take a minute and talk about this."

She didn't really have a choice. Finding out what he was up to would be a good idea. Would probably save her some grief later.

"You sit down and start talking, and I'll listen." She gestured to the seat behind him. "You have two minutes. Starting now."

He didn't look happy at her high-handedness but he didn't argue. He sat, stretched out those long legs and waited for her to join him. He motioned to the empty seat next to him.

"Let's have it," she prompted, hating herself for noticing every little detail about him, such as those long legs. She wasn't getting any closer. No way.

"We're actually after the same thing here," he confessed. "You simply don't realize it yet."

Big surprise. "Who're you working for?" He was no longer affiliated with Interpol. That didn't leave a lot of margin on this side of the line between good and evil.

"I'm afraid I can't divulge that information."

A choked laugh burst out of her. "You have to be kidding."

He flared those long-fingered hands. "Afraid not. Your security clearance isn't high enough."

"I have the highest—"

He pressed a finger to his lips.

Total meltdown threatened.

She struggled to make her trigger finger relax.

"It's hardly fair for me to expect you to feel comfortable under the circumstances," he allowed unabashedly, "but you know how this works, Sabrina. Duty must come first."

"Stop calling me Sabrina."

She wanted to kick herself for allowing him to hear how angry the sound of her name on his lips made her. He didn't need to know how badly he'd hurt her. He didn't deserve to know, damn him.

He held up his hands in a show of surrender. "I apologize, Agent Fox, but we don't have a lot of time here. We need an exit strategy."

The man had clearly lost his mind.

"I'm not going anywhere with you, Drake. I have my orders, and they don't include you." She reached behind her for the door, careful not to take her eyes off him. "Now, if you'll excuse me, I have to go."

"Wait!"

The fluid way he lunged to his feet should have had her disengaging the safety on her weapon; instead, she found herself studying the move, drinking in the grace she'd always marveled at.

"We have to get off this train. If they catch us, we're dead."

The need to kick herself was nearly over-whelming. She had to be losing her grip. Why hadn't she walked out already? "There is no *we*, Drake. I have my mission, you have yours. End of story."

He moved closer, too close. "Right now, *you* are my mission."

She could have done without the way he lowered his deep, resonating voice or the way he looked at her…as if he cared.

Yeah, right.

"You know, Drake, I might have been a fool once, but don't expect me to make the same mistake again. Whatever your scam, I'm out of here."

"Just give me a couple of hours," he persisted, "that's all I'm asking for. Once we're off this train and out of danger, we'll figure out where we go from there. I'm telling you the truth here."

Why didn't he get it? There was no *we!*

Sabrina shoved the weapon back into her boot and shouldered into her jacket. She was done here. "I wish I could say it was nice to see you again, but that would be a lie." He looked as if he were about to reach out to touch her, but she gave him a pointed look. "Don't even think about it. This conversation is over."

That was when he did the last thing she'd expected.

In another of those fluid, mesmerizing moves, he drew his own weapon and aimed it at her. "I didn't want to have to do it this way, but unfortunately you've left me no alternative."

She had been a fool twice. Her foolish heart had reacted as if he hadn't betrayed her once already. As if he hadn't walked away two years ago and never looked back. She was an idiot.

"Let's stay cool. We'll exit east and make our way to the luggage car."

He'd said he needed an exit strategy. Personally, she had no desire to jump from a train moving at this speed, but, evidently, the choice wouldn't be up to her. Oh, well. Maybe she'd get lucky and he'd break something—like his neck.

"Whatever you say." She held up her hands in surrender.

"First, I'll need your weapons."

With a huff of exasperation, she reached into her boot and extricated the .22. When she'd passed it to him, she went for her bag.

"I'll get that one." He pushed her hand away from her bag and reached inside.

Damn, just when she'd made up her mind to go for the pen that Big Hugh had given her. She would have loved to put him down like the horse's ass he was.

Drake tucked the 9mm into his waistband at the small of his back, and stuffed the .22 into his jacket pocket. He slid his own 9mm into his waistband, as well, this one in the front.

"You always did need a prop, didn't you, Drake?" She glanced pointedly at the weapon filling out the front of his jeans. If she were a man, a Glock was the last weapon she would want that close to the family jewels.

He manacled her arm and ushered her to the door. "I'm certain you recall quite vividly how well equipped I am, Fox, but now isn't the time to reminisce."

Humiliation burned her cheeks.

The urge to do bodily injury had her balling her hands into fists.

"Shall we?" He indicated the door.

"After you." She wasn't about to make this easy for him.

He checked the corridor and then ushered her out the door.

The idea that he was working as a private contractor now fit perfectly with the kind of agent he'd been. He had never played by the rules. She should have seen him for what he was three years ago, before she'd fallen in love with him. An arrogant, self-centered, self-serving—

"You look great, Fox."

That he whispered the remark close to her ear

when she was forced to stop for other passengers exiting their compartments made her want to turn around and punch him square in the gut.

When an elderly couple had strolled down the corridor, Sabrina resumed her forward movement. She refused to be baited.

Her indifference did nothing but fuel his determination. As they moved into the passenger cars, he cozied up behind her. The movement in and out of seats by the other passengers prevented her from putting some distance between them.

"I like your hair longer."

It wasn't that much longer. Maybe a couple of inches.

She paused while a mother attempted to drag her toddler from a seat to go to the bathroom.

"That new scent you're wearing," he whispered against her hair, "it's very pleasing."

She shivered in spite of herself.

Enough.

She executed a one-eighty, putting herself nose to nose with him. "Back off, Drake."

Again he held up both hands and adopted a look of innocence.

"*Excusez-moi*," the mother who'd managed to get her child into the aisle said.

"*Excusez-moi*." Sabrina stepped to one side so that the lady and her kid could pass.

Drake did the same, except he somehow

managed to gift the lady with a smile charming enough to have her blushing as she dragged her kid past him.

Sabrina pivoted and headed forward once more. Why had he shown back up in her life? What did he want? Besides the codes, obviously? After all, that was her mission.

Maybe he wanted nothing.

Maybe he just wanted to use her again.

That was not going to happen a second time. She'd go along with his game until she uncovered exactly what he was up to, and then she'd take him down.

If he wasn't working for the U.S. government or the British government, then he was an enemy. Pure and simple. It was her duty to see that he failed to complete his mission. As long, of course, as it didn't interfere with her own.

The very idea that he would claim to be here looking out for her was ludicrous. He'd fooled her once; he wouldn't get that chance again.

First and foremost, she had to stay focused. She had to intercept that courier. She needed those codes before they left this country.

They reached the luggage car. The entrance was secured. He reached into the interior pocket of his jacket and removed a key. Once inside the car, he secured the door and went straight to the sliding side door used for loading and unloading the car.

"If you think I'm jumping from this train, you've lost your mind."

He glanced over his shoulder at her. "In approximately ten minutes, there's an intersection transfer. The train will slow down to a minimal speed. That's when we'll make our move."

"No way, Drake. I'm staying on this train until I get where I'm going. No negotiations." She looked back at the door. "I'll take my chances with the *other* bad guys, thank you very much."

He didn't respond until he'd prepped the large sliding door for easy opening. He intended to be prepared when the time came. Too bad he'd have to make his move without her. The only way she was bailing off this train was if he shot her first.

His attention shifted to her once more. "Oh, I see how it is. You're still holding a grudge against me for that final mission."

"Gee, how'd you guess?"

He'd used her two years ago. They'd been selected for a joint mission to steal a much-needed list from an enemy once employed by the infamous Russian KGB. When things had gone wrong, he'd made her a patsy by allowing her to be captured to distract the enemy while he made the big save.

Drake had come out looking like a hero and she had come off looking like an incompetent fool. And if all that hadn't been bad enough, he'd slept with the enemy's female confidante to get the damned list while she was tortured for information on whom she was working with. Of course, he'd saved her in the end once his first priority was accomplished—getting the list.

In retrospect, his tactics likely salvaged what clearly would have been an unwinnable mission. Technically, they had been on the same team, so the end should have justified the means. Somehow, it hadn't.

"I did what I had to do," he said with absolutely no remorse. "It was the only way, and you know it. Retrieving that list was essential."

That compulsion to slug him swamped her again. "I understand that, Agent Drake. I really do. But I think sleeping with the other woman was just a tad over the top, don't you?"

Her breath caught at the flicker of regret she saw in those blue eyes. She told herself she'd imagined it, but had she?

"You would have done the same in my shoes," he argued. "It was part of the job. There was nothing pleasurable about it."

How foolish of her. Of course, she'd imagined the regret. This was a man who had no compunction whatsoever about screwing anyone over. Renewed outrage roared through her, but she'd be damned if she'd let him see it. "You know what, you're probably right. We have nothing else to discuss. We're not working together anymore. We're not even friends. So whatever you're doing here, Drake, as far as I'm concerned this little reunion is over."

Temporary insanity, that was all it could have been. She should never have allowed him to drag her into whatever game he was playing. Shooting him back there in that compartment would have been a much better option.

"I want my weapons back." She held out her hand.

He stared at her, then at her hand. Just when she was sure he wasn't going to cooperate, he placed the 9mm in her outstretched palm. She shoved it back into her purse and held out her hand for the .22.

"Did you forget something?" she prompted.

"Sorry." He fished the .22 out of his pocket and gave it back to her.

"Goodbye, Drake."

She gave him her back and headed for the door.

"They'll never allow you off this train alive."

She told herself to keep walking, to go out that door and never look back. But she couldn't let it go so easily.

Sabrina faced him once more, anger blurring her logic. "And you would care one way or the other whether or not I survive? Is that what you're trying to say?"

She wanted to see the lie in his eyes when he

opened that perfect mouth again. She needed to see the lie. It was the only way to keep hating him. The only way to protect herself.

For two years she had nurtured the bitterness and the sheer hatred. How could it vanish so damned easily in his presence?

It just wasn't fair, dammit.

"Of course I care." He moved a step in her direction but kept his hands at his sides. "Sabrina, if you believe nothing else, believe me when I say—"

"Save it, Drake." She shook her head. "I'm out of here."

"Don't open that door, Sabrina," he warned. "They could be right outside. We should jump while we still can. You must believe me when I say—"

"The only thing I must do," she returned bluntly, "is get away from you." She turned away from him and reached for the door.

The door abruptly burst open, sending her stumbling back.

"Don't move!"

The muzzle of a weapon thrust into her face.

"Get your hands up."

The order came from a goon holding a .45 and was directed beyond her shoulder. To Drake, she imagined. Two more men entered around the goon who now stared down the barrel at her, the glint in his eyes warning that he didn't have a problem with blowing a hole through her chest.

"Well, well," the guy with the .45 mused, "I finally get to meet the celebrated Agent Sabrina Fox." He surveyed her from head to toe and back. "Your official photos don't do you justice, lass." He glanced past Sabrina. "Put him down."

When she turned in an attempt to do something to stop them, the butt of the .45 slammed against her skull.

The last thing she saw was Drake on his knees with a muzzle rammed against his forehead.

Dammit.

She hated him. Hated every damned thing about him, from those amazing eyes to his great lips to his broad shoulders.

But she didn't want him to die this way.

She wanted to kill him herself.

It wasn't fair that someone else got to do it.

CHAPTER TEN

THE TRAIN WAS still moving when Sabrina stirred.

Pain shattered in the left side of her skull right behind her ear.

Bastard.

The goon with the .45 probably given her a mild contusion.

She told her eyes to open, but they refused. She needed to assess her situation and she couldn't do that with her eyes closed.

With a little more prodding, her eyelids fluttered open.

That simple movement sent pain exploding behind her eyes.

Damn.

When the pain had settled, she tried again.

Slowly, just a crack at first. Then she blinked.

Darkness greeted her.

For what must have been a minute, maybe more, she lay there, careful not to move, allowing her senses to absorb her environment.

Dark. Still moving, but the movement was different, not so smooth. The sound wasn't the same. Not that perpetual hum; more of a roar. And the smell. She filled her lungs, let it out slowly. Closed up, stinky, like a guy's locker room.

Using extreme caution, she attempted to move her arms. Her right hand came up to touch her head. The spot on her scalp where the butt of the .45 had landed was tender as hell, but she didn't feel any dampness or stickiness. Maybe she was lucky, there was no blood.

She tried to move her left hand, but she couldn't lift it. Uncertainty sent panic twisting through her. Wait. She wiggled her hand and arm but couldn't move it beyond a certain point. Now she understood. She was tethered to something with a thin plastic band or what felt like a plastic band. Her feet were unrestrained as far as she could tell. That was good.

Mainly, she was just glad to be alive.

Drake.

Adrenaline rushed through her veins, making her head spin and throb.

Did those men kill him?

She sat up.

Groaned with the agony of movement.

She should have listened to him. He'd warned her that someone on the train was after her. She hadn't listened and she'd gotten them both captured.

She jerked her bound wrist, wanted to get free so she could explore her dark prison. She needed to see if Drake was in here with her…if he was still alive.

Dammit. He was never wrong when it came to outmaneuvering the enemy. Damn her for not listening.

She tried to remember if the weapon pointed at Drake had fired before she lost consciousness. She did not want him to be dead. At least not like that. There was more she wanted to say to him.

Okay, she had to calm down. She couldn't think about that right now.

A change in forward momentum sent her hurtling against the floor again.

What the hell?

Then she got it.

She was in a truck or van or something moving along a highway. The driver had just braked hard for a turn or a stop.

Okay. She was definitely not on the train anymore.

She peered through the darkness, couldn't see a damned thing.

If she could get loose, she could at least feel around for some sort of weapon. When this journey ended, she'd be in deep trouble if she wasn't prepared.

The fact that the man who'd given her the knock on the head had recognized her, had made reference to her reputation, was significant. She just didn't know how yet. Drake's saying she had been targeted for elimination, but she wasn't about to believe that just now. Still, in the back of her mind she couldn't help considering that someone had broken into her apartment and followed her—just yesterday.

Okay, focus. Right now, escaping these thugs had to be her top priority.

Taking her time, she used her free hand to investigate the area around her. The floor felt cold, like metal. It was ridged, not smooth. Behind her was what felt like a wall. She struggled to her feet. The wall or whatever it was continued well above her head.

She moved as far in each direction as she could and found a similar wall on either side of her. A panel truck, maybe. Too large for a van or a pickup.

With her hand tethered to the wall behind her, she couldn't hope to move forward very far, but she gave it a try. She'd gotten maybe five feet when she encountered an object on the floor.

She nudged it with the toe of her boot.

Oh, hell.

A body.

She dropped to her knees, her left arm stretched behind her in an uncomfortable manner. Moving her right hand slowly over the form, she first identified the jacket. Leather. Bomber jacket.

Her heart skipped an irrational beat.

Her fingers moved up to the face and her stomach turned over with relief.

Drake.

She would know those damned lips anywhere. And the perfect nose.

Holding her breath, she placed her palm over the center of his chest and waited for the rise and fall that would indicate he was still breathing. Three seconds passed and finally it happened. The air filled his lungs, expanding his chest, and relief rushed through her all over again.

But that didn't mean he wasn't injured.

She took a moment to gather her wits, then performed a more thorough examination with her one free hand.

No blood on his face...no indication of damage that she could feel. A hell of a lump just behind his right temple told her he'd gotten the same treatment she had. She felt inside his jacket, moving her hand over his chest, along his sides and down the length of one leg. It wasn't easy to make the reach, but she managed. Her hand moved slowly up the other leg, encountering no dampness or palpable indication of injury.

Using all her might, she pulled him toward her and onto his side. When she'd checked his back for injury and found nothing, she felt satisfied.

He was alive.

That meant she still had a chance of killing him herself.

She let the realization that vengeance was still a possibility wash over her.

Mostly she was just glad he wasn't dead.

The way he'd betrayed her two years ago hadn't been personal; on some level she knew that. He'd done whatever necessary to get the job done. And maybe he was right. Maybe she would have done the same.

Still, it hurt.

She had to stop obsessing about the past.

When she'd composed herself, she searched his pockets. Whatever he'd carried had been removed, save for a comb and his wallet that were useless to her at the moment. She needed a knife.

What about her purse?

Taking her time, she moved over every square foot of the floor that her tether would allow her to reach. And there it was, in the corner, turned upside down. Both weapons as well as her cell phone were missing of course. But the brush was there.

Thank you, Hugh.

She squeezed the handle until the blade slid from its hiding place. Bracing her back against the wall so that she didn't sway with any change in momentum, she slid the blade between her wrist and the binding. The band was tight, one wrong slice and she could be the one in need of medical attention. She sawed the blade back and forth. It took some time, but the restraining strap eventually popped loose.

She rubbed her wrist and then scooted back over to where Drake lay, not moving.

He hadn't stirred. That could be a bad sign. Although she felt no indication of injury, there could be internal damage.

She checked his hands again, but he wasn't restrained in the same manner she had been. His bindings were around his ankles. Again, something plastic. Reminded her of the disposable cuffs cops used. Impossible to get loose without a knife.

Taking her time, making sure she didn't slice into skin, she cut through the bindings.

She pushed the blade back inside the brush and placed it on the floor next to her. She might need it again before this was over, though she wasn't sure it would be much help in hand-to-hand combat with the odds four to one. Those particular odds seemed to be showing up a lot lately.

"Drake." She shook him gently. "Wake up."

He groaned.

Good sign.

Several more shakes later, he finally spoke. "Are you all right?"

She told herself not to put too much stock in the idea that he asked about her first. Probably just habit.

"I'm good. How about you?"

He pushed up to a sitting position. "Other than a raging headache, I'm quite grand."

She doubted he was quite grand, but at least he was able to crack a joke.

"Do you have any idea where we are?"

"Me first," she interjected, overriding his determination to take control of the situation. He always did that. Just like Ledger. What was it about these guys that made them think they had to be in charge? The idea that Interpol was chomping at the bit to take over field ops in IT&PA flashed through her mind. She wondered if Drake knew anything about that. Marx had spoken as if Drake would have been the one chosen to run IT&PA two years ago. "Do you know who these people are?"

"No. Only that whoever is in charge wants you, dead or alive. I wish you'd listened to me and we would have gotten off that train without all this fanfare."

She ignored his jab and winced when a frown attempted to nag at her brow. The idea that this team wanted her dead could only mean one thing—whoever was in charge was someone she'd done business with before. Someone who'd taken their business personally and wanted revenge. But how could anyone have known she would be on this mission? Who had sold her out?

As much as Drake's assessment appeared to be on the mark, that still didn't explain how he had come into possession of this knowledge. There were a hell of a lot of questions she needed answered.

"And you would know this how?"

"I can't reveal my sources. You know that."

Well, hell. So he was going to play it that way, was he?

"That's your choice." She got to her feet, swayed a bit, as much from the movement of the vehicle as from her knock on the head. She needed to find a way out of here that didn't include getting herself killed or both legs broken.

She moved to the side wall and felt her way to the other end of their prison. Since what felt like two towering doors made up this end, the other end was likely the closest to the cab of the vehicle.

If she attempted to open these doors, one of two things could happen. She'd find them locked or she'd go flying out onto the highway, risking death on impact or from another vehicle running her over.

She needed a way to hang on before she attempted that kind of move.

Moving to the corner where the door met the side wall, she fumbled around for any sort of grab bar. Something made for tying down a load. She found nothing.

She'd just have to take her chances.

Waiting until they reached their destination was far too risky.

Taking a deep breath, she pushed down on the lever she assumed to be part of the door's operating mechanism. It didn't budge. She pushed harder. Nothing.

So maybe she needed to pull upward.

She pulled.

The lever moved a fraction of an inch.

She pulled harder still.

The door flew open, wrenching the lever out of her hand and dragging her forward.

Strong arms banded around her waist and yanked her backward.

Pain bounced around in her skull as she landed in a heap on the floor with Drake.

Sunlight streamed in through the open door. She blinked at the brightness of it.

The road was empty behind them.

She scrambled onto all fours and surveyed the passing landscape in an attempt to get her bearings.

Trees. Lots of trees. Heavy undergrowth. They had to be miles from the city. Miles from where they'd been taken from the train.

She'd like to know how that happened. Maybe their captors had kept them on the train until the next stop.

"We need to be ready," she said to Drake. "If

this truck slows for a turn, we should jump and hope for the best."

"Excellent plan."

Definitely as good as his suggestion to jump from the train, she thought.

Together, with him still holding on to her, they scooted closer to the door.

This close, his scent played havoc with her senses. As dank-smelling as the truck was and with the wind whipping through it now, it seemed impossible that she could pick his scent out of the mix, but somehow she could.

Memories of the year they'd spent practically living together filtered through her mind, making her wish she could forget. But no matter how she'd tried, she'd never been able to put him completely out of her mind.

He just wasn't the kind of guy a girl could forget.

Even when it was in her best interest.

"Feels like old times," he said.

Maybe a little too much so. She scooted away from him, broke the contact. "This isn't anything like old times, Drake. We're not on the same team."

She didn't look at him. She needed to stay focused. The moment for escape could come and go in the blink of an eye. She had to be ready.

"You're involved with someone?"

The idea that he would even have the nerve to ask ticked her off. "That's none of your business."

"True." He pulled the lapels of his coat closer together to block the cold and wind. "Just thought we might pass the time with a little chitchat."

"Chitchat is something you do with friends, Drake." She wished she knew where her coat was. "We're not friends."

He glanced around their moving prison before taking off toward the other end. He came back before she bothered to check out what he was up to.

Draping her coat around her shoulders, he noted, "We used to be friends."

"That was before you betrayed me." She jammed her arms through the sleeves and hugged the coat around her. She wanted to bite off her tongue for bringing that whole betrayal thing up again. It only made her sound as if she still cared. He'd already explained the reason he'd done what he had. Pretending she didn't understand revealed her emotional turmoil.

His silence only added to his guilt, in her opinion. She might be obsessing, but he was guilty. He could at least apologize or offer some sort of excuse other than it was his job. Too much wine or temporary insanity.

Anything.

But he didn't.

"You see anything familiar?"

So he wanted to talk, just not about the past.

"No."

"How is Director Marx?"

Retiring.

That reality slammed into her like a raging bull coming at a matador. She ached as if she'd been gored. He was her mentor, almost a father to her, as clichéd as that sounded. She couldn't imagine life at IT&PA without him.

But she wouldn't share any of that with Drake. If she couldn't tell the members of her team, she damned sure wasn't going to tell Drake.

"He's fine."

There wasn't a lot of conviction in her words. She hoped that he took her tone as showing her indifference toward him. She didn't want him reading anything into what she had to say.

The truck abruptly braked.

Anticipation shot through her veins.

She scooted down to the open door and prayed that with the sudden change in the vehicle's momentum the door wouldn't flop into the view of the driver's side mirror. A very real possibility.

Sure enough, the truck slowed for a right turn. The door flew open wider.

If the driver saw it…

"Jump!"

She ignored Drake, checked the road for other vehicles. It was still clear.

"Jump! Now!" he repeated.

She should have listened to him on the train.
Why the hell was she hesitating now?

She jumped.

She hit the shoulder of the road on all fours,
then tumbled into the ditch. Drake landed not two
feet from her in a similarly awkward manner.

They lay still, hoping like hell the truck would
keep going. The ground was icy and her head
throbbed incessantly.

The squeal of brakes warned that the driver had
spotted the open door.

"We have to run for it." She sprang to her feet,
keeping her head low.

"Agreed."

Drake headed for the tree line. She followed.

Shouts from the truck echoed in the frigid air.
The driver had traveled about another hundred
yards before recognizing that something was
wrong.

Not much of a head start for them, but it was
better than nothing.

Sabrina cursed her boots as she tore through the
woods right behind Drake.

Her left heel broke loose, sending her pitching
forward.

She tried to catch herself.

Didn't happen.

She hit the ground hard. The breath whooshed
out of her lungs.

"Dammit!"

She scrambled up, then hissed another curse at her boot as she hobbled forward.

"Let me see," Drake said.

She started to argue, but there was no time. She sat down on the ground. He crouched next to her and checked the sole of her left boot. The heel had snapped off. He grasped her right foot and broke the heel off that boot.

"That should work."

He stood, then pulled her to her feet.

She probably should have thanked him, but she didn't. No time, she told herself. But that was a lie.

Barreling through the trees, she tuned out his presence. Outrunning those goons after them was their only chance of escape. Since she and Drake were unarmed, a face-off with the goons was out of the question. Since they were outnumbered two to one, a hand-to-hand battle carried unfavorable odds.

Running was the best chance they had of surviving.

She let the adrenaline fuel her. She allowed the flight instinct to guide her through the rugged terrain. Limbs scraped at her legs. Holes and rocks caused her to stumble time and time again, but she didn't slow down…didn't let up.

She'd made a promise to Marx.

No way was she going to die on this mission.

Whatever the enemy's agenda, the one thing a spy could count on in the end if captured was death.

She had no intention of dying today.

"This way."

Drake grabbed her hand and dragged her to the left. The terrain sloped sharply toward a valley.

Beyond the woods, she got the occasional glimpse of what looked like a house and maybe farmland.

Rows and rows of dormant grapes spread out beyond the trees.

Several buildings—a winery, she realized—dotted the landscape.

They'd reached the closest building when three men burst from the tree line back up the hill they'd just descended.

Sabrina flattened against the building just beyond the corner facing the men tearing down the slope.

Her heart pounded. Her lungs heaved in an attempt to drag in more air.

She and Drake had to hide.

Outrunning the enemy was no longer a viable option.

Outsmarting them was the only alternative left.

"Follow me."

Drake didn't ask any questions. Probably because the bad guys had reached the edge of the vineyard. Apparently he didn't have any better idea.

The first building housed equipment and not much else. Inside, the smell of oil and grease reminded her of the garage where she'd taken her car for servicing back in high school.

She cracked the door just far enough to peer out. Moving to the next building could prove hazardous since the enemy was close by.

Oh yeah. Three of the four men entered her line of vision.

"They're here." She glanced at Drake. "This is where it happens."

He nodded.

Their only choice now was to arm themselves with whatever they could find.

Sabrina grabbed what looked like a steel pipe but was most likely some sort of tool. The only thing she needed the pipe to connect with was the head of one or two of those jerks.

Pipe in hand, she made her way between two tractors and crouched behind the large rear wheels of one. She edged in as deeply as possible between the wheel and the tractor body. From her position, she couldn't see much, but she was well hidden. With the low lighting, spotting her would be difficult.

Drake had taken a position, as well. She wasn't sure where, but he was as skilled, or maybe more so, than she was at evading the enemy. He could take care of himself. Right now was definitely an every-man-for-himself scenario.

The door opened. Sunlight poured across the dirt floor but didn't quite reach her position.

She breathed a little easier.

The three men spoke in French as they spread out to search for their targets. Their curt conversation provided no additional intelligence, just snapped commands of who was to look where. Which could prove useful. The idea that the men took no precautions in the way of stealth indicated they weren't concerned as to their ability to overtake their targets.

Not a good sign.

Generally when capture was the intent, stealth was immensely important. Pursuing the element of surprise ensured the likelihood of disabling a target. If these men weren't concerned with catching their targets off guard, then they most likely had orders to simply eliminate, rather than capture.

Footsteps near her position sent a new band of tension curling around Sabrina's chest. Her fingers tightened around her pipe. What she would give for that .22 or even the pen just now.

"Ici!"

Scuffling sounds echoed from the other side of the building.

She heard the blast of a weapon.

Damn.

They'd found Drake's hiding place.

Sabrina eased out of her own hiding place.

The man who'd come so close to her position had turned to see what was happening with his buddies.

Too bad for him.

Sabrina swung the pipe, connecting directly with his head.

He crumpled to the ground.

She focused, slowed her heart rate, and listened to the sounds of the ongoing engagement as she crouched down and lifted the downed man's weapon. A Glock .40 cal. Perfect. She shoved it into her coat pocket as she got back to her feet.

The sound of fists connecting with flesh. Groans. Curses. Drake was giving someone a run for his money.

But where was the third man?

"Don't move."

The nudge of a muzzle into the back of her skull answered her question.

The third man was right behind her.

CHAPTER ELEVEN

THE THIRD GUY reclaimed his comrade's weapon and then shoved Sabrina out into the open area near the front of the building.

He shouted something she didn't catch and the sounds of fighting abruptly subsided.

Great. She had to go and get caught, and now Drake would have no choice but to surrender in order to save her. Just great. Just like two years ago all over again, only that time he had purposely caused her to get caught.

Drake, his hands up in the air, walked out into the open. The guy he'd beaten the crap out of, considering his bloody face, followed, his weapon boring into Drake's back. So far, the guy she'd put down hadn't gotten back up. If she was lucky, he wouldn't.

At least his absence leveled the playing field to some degree.

Drake's gaze met hers and she couldn't help sending a message of apology. No one liked being the reason for capture, most especially her.

She'd let the enemy sneak up on her. That hadn't happened in years.

Somehow she felt certain this was Drake's fault. He'd screwed up her instincts and her timing.

He'd always been bad for her.

"Sur vos genoux!"

Her attention snapped back to the present as the man ordered Drake to his knees.

Oh, hell. Here they went again. Drake had survived the last time he'd been forced into an execution stance; she hoped like hell he would end up as lucky this time.

Drake's gaze met hers once more just before he dropped to his knees. The look there was unmistakable.

He intended to make a move.

And why not? He was dead anyway.

"Hey, dirtbag," she shouted at the guy with the 9mm trained on the back of Drake's head. "Aren't you going to help your friend? He's bleeding to death over there. I tried my best to kill him."

The guy behind her jammed the muzzle of his gun hard into her skull. But that didn't matter. What mattered was the split second she'd bought Drake.

When the man towering over Drake made the mistake of shifting his attention to her, Drake bolted into a blur of action.

He twisted, moving from the line of fire and at the same time jamming his elbow into the guy's crotch.

The weapon discharged into the dirt.

The man, screaming curses, curled into the fetal position on the ground. Drake recovered the weapon he'd dropped.

A powerful arm banded around her throat and jerked her against the rigid body behind her. The guy took aim at Drake and shouted for him to drop his weapon.

Sabrina knocked her captor's arm upward as the weapon discharged. She braced her left leg in front of his and threw her full body weight in that direction. The two tumbled to the ground. The weapon fired again. She was face down in the dirt. Her captor was on top of her. His arm tightened on her throat. She kicked and scratched. Sank her teeth into his forearm.

He screamed. His arm loosened.

She twisted around to face him just in time to push the weapon away from her head. The recoil and the blast from a third round being discharged sent her heart lunging into her throat.

The guy's weight suddenly lifted.

Drake jerked him upright by the hair of his head. The weapon went flying.

By the time Sabrina got to her feet, the guy lay on the ground unmoving. Sometime during her struggle he'd rendered the other man unconscious as well.

Drake wiped the blood from his lips. "We should check their IDs and get out of here."

Sabrina nodded in agreement. She didn't recognize any of the men, but a name could be useful later in tracking down who had hired them.

"Take a look at this."

Drake was looking at the contents of the wallet belonging to the first man she'd downed. He held up an ID card. "He's American."

Sabrina looked at the name. Caleb Shooks. What the hell?

Drake tossed the wallet onto the man's body. "We should make sure they don't have friends close by."

Putting aside the fact that one of the enemy was American for the moment, Sabrina rushed to the door and checked for movement or sound outside. If the vineyard owners or any of their employees were around, they would likely have heard the gunfire.

Nothing moved. No sound.

Seemed strange that no one was around, but she didn't have time to analyze the situation.

Drake came up behind her. "Clear?"

"Yeah."

"Perhaps we should secure these gentlemen."

She glanced back over her shoulder at the two lying in the dirt. He was right. They needed all the time they could buy, and killing them would be an abuse of power. Even if it was damned tempting.

He handed her the Glock. "I know it's your favorite."

She refused to smile as she accepted the weapon. He'd tucked a 9mm Beretta into his jeans. "Let's get this done."

Drake located a spool of twine and a utility knife. He took care of the two men up front while she secured the man she'd knocked unconscious with the pipe. She kept mulling over the fact that he was American. She told herself that Americans could be the enemy sometimes…but this felt different somehow. Being followed back home in New York and having her apartment broken into keep nagging at her. This couldn't be connected.

That was crazy.

Outside, the cold wind reminded her that December was not the best time to tour a vineyard in France. She surveyed the landscape. Still no sign of any other human presence.

Her gaze landed on a truck parked near the house.

"Transportation would be nice." Really nice, she considered, shivering in her crippled boots.

Judging by the sun, it was well past noon. She needed to get to Troyes. She didn't know how far off course this jaunt had taken her, but covering ground quickly was essential.

"Check the house, I'll check the truck."

She jogged over to the house. Checked a couple

of windows. If anyone was home, there was no in-dication. Strangely enough, the front door was unlocked. She moved as quietly as possible through the rooms. Empty.

In the bedroom she checked the closet, grabbed a pair of jeans and shoes. The jeans were a size too small, but she'd get them on one way or another. The shoes seemed about right. Black leather, lace-up. They looked a little like bowling shoes. The Parisian version of sneakers, she surmised.

Close enough.

Outside Drake already had the truck running. She jumped into the passenger seat and he took off.

She peeled off the boots and tights, then wiggled out of the skirt.

"Keep your eyes on the road," she said to Drake when she caught him looking her way.

"What can I say? I have a thing for silk and lace."

She remembered all too well how he felt about silk and lace. "Shut up and drive."

The jeans slid up onto her hips with no problem and, surprisingly, buttoned fairly easily, as well. Either she'd lost weight or the size ran a little large.

She wished for thick, warm socks as she laced up the shoes. But there hadn't been time to dig around for anything else.

The landscape captured her attention briefly—rolling hills and a church spire towering high above a village nestled against the foothills in the distance. Quaint beauty, with the rolling hills of wine country as a backdrop. It was enough to make a woman forget about her aches and pains from recent battle…for a minute or two.

She grimaced as reality came back into vivid focus. Her head throbbed. Her knees were scraped. Her throat was bruised.

Still, she'd come out better off than Drake. His lip was busted. His cheek would likely be bruised and swollen. His knuckles were bloody, and he moved stiffly enough for her to recognize he'd taken some powerful blows to his trunk.

Her gaze lingered on the long fingers clenched around the steering wheel. She'd always had a thing for his hands. Nice hands. Strong and steady. Thorough in their work as well as their play.

She blinked and looked away.

Where in the world had that insane thought come from?

That knock on the head had obviously rattled her brain.

"What's our destination?"

She looked away from him. "Troyes."

Her instincts went immediately on point. No matter that he'd helped her escape those men, he was still as much the enemy as they had been.

She needed to get to Troyes, but that was all the information he would get.

If those codes got out of the country before she could intercept the courier...

She didn't want to think about that just yet.

"You know those codes will be way out of your reach by now," Drake offered as if she'd voiced her concerns out loud.

"I don't know what you're talking about."

He wasn't on her side. He was apparently a private contractor now. She had to keep that in mind. Even if their past wasn't enough to have her on guard around him, that fact would be more than sufficient.

"Just as well," he commented, nonchalantly. "The best place to intercept is at the final destination in any event."

She tamped down her interest. Refused to let him see that he'd nudged her curiosity.

When she didn't take the bait, he said, "Good thing I know the final destination."

Determined not to be drawn into whatever his scam might be, she leaned back in the seat and enjoyed the landscape.

The sun was dropping fast. She'd almost forgotten how early it got dark in Europe during the dead of winter. By four or four-fifteen, it would be damned dark. And cold. She pulled her coat more tightly around her.

She considered the village in the distance once more. Parting ways with Drake would be in her best interest. Maybe when they reached the village she'd do just that. She didn't have any ID or money, but she had contacts. All she needed was a phone.

She didn't need him, and she sure didn't trust him.

The truck suddenly surged forward; then the engine choked down as if it might die.

"Oh, bugger."

Her attention shot to Drake. "What's the problem?" Dammit, she needed to get to Troyes. She'd lost too much time already.

"We're out of petrol."

He guided the sputtering truck onto the side of the road. The instant he tapped the brake, the engine died with a slow coughing sound.

"Look at it this way." He nodded toward the road ahead of them. "It's not that far to the village. We should make it by dark."

Somehow she didn't find that knowledge comforting.

She got out of the truck, dug around in her coat pockets for her gloves and tugged them on. A scarf would be nice about now, but she no longer had one. Hugging the coat more closely around her, she headed toward the village in the distance.

"I really hate to be a drag, Fox." Drake hustled up next to her. "But I'm confident it would be in our best interest to stay clear of the road since we're now on foot."

He was right, loath though she was to admit it. Since they had only encountered three men in the equipment shed back there, the fourth guy had probably gone in search of his pals by now. They could be headed this way already, for all Sabrina knew. Staying out of sight would be imperative. She surveyed the terrain off the road.

And a hell of a lot slower going.

Damn. She would lose more time.

But being late was preferable to being dead.

The countryside was made up of rolling hills, clumps of wooded areas and acres and acres of well-cultivated vineyards.

All they had to do was stay in the fringes of the trees and rows of dormant grape vines.

At least she had the right shoes for the trek.

They'd walked maybe twenty minutes in blissful silence before Drake said, "There's a rumor that changes are in store for your organization."

Now how would he know about that? she wondered.

"I'm afraid that information is classified." A smile toyed with the corners of her mouth. She liked knowing something he didn't. She liked even more that it would stick in his craw.

"I'm not so sure Ledger is the right man for the job, however."

She stopped, stared at him. "How the hell do you know that?"

He shrugged, looking entirely too smug. "I didn't. I told you there were rumors." The uninjured corner of his mouth lifted in a lopsided grin. "Thanks for the confirmation."

She wanted to scream! Instead, she stormed off through the trees. She wasn't saying another word, no matter what. Then again, she shouldn't be surprised. She'd gotten the distinct impression from her last conversation with Marx that Drake would have been the one to take over IT&PA two years ago. There was a time when she would have considered that a good thing. Like Marx, Drake had been a man of honor, a man of total dedication.

Her thoughts about him had changed drastically two years ago.

"Ledger always had a thing for you, you know. But he isn't really your type, is he?"

With her lips pressed firmly together, she stared straight ahead. She wouldn't give him the satisfaction of knowing that he was right. As charming and handsome as Ledger was, he wasn't her type.

Her type was…more aggressive and ambitious in a more physical sense. Ledger was more the executive type. The guy who took charge of planning and research. Not really the man in the field, though he'd done his time in the field. She couldn't imagine him with a bloody lip or a bruised jaw. He always looked perfect. Never a hair out of place. Never stuck his foot in his mouth. Perfect manners. Perfect everything.

Too perfect.

"That's what I thought."

She couldn't believe Drake had the audacity to answer his own questions. Answering for her at that. He didn't know her anymore. He had no idea what she liked or didn't like these days.

"Ledger is too calm for you. Too organized."

Ignore him, Sabrina. He's baiting you, she thought to herself.

"You prefer a man who thinks by the seat of his pants. Who isn't afraid to jump into the fray and get his hands dirty. You like your men assertive and determined. A man who acts first and asks questions later."

Her jaw had started to pulse with tension from the hard set of her teeth. She would not let him drag her into this conversation. Just let him keep talking to himself. He seemed to be doing pretty damned good at both asking and answering his questions.

"He's probably really lousy in bed. Too much a linear thinker to be impulsive."

Sabrina stopped again. She waited until he looked at her before she spoke. It was important that she see his eyes when she made her statement. "Gee, Drake, you've really put a lot of thought into what kind of lover Ledger is. Are you sure you're not the one who's interested in him?"

A muscle in his jaw started to twitch, but he said nothing.

"That's what I thought." With that Sabrina continued her march forward. At least now maybe he'd keep his mouth shut for a while.

She could use the peace and quiet.

To her dismay, Drake's comments had gotten under her skin exactly the way he'd intended.

How could he know that Ledger was being considered for a position at IT&PA? Who could he be working for that would allow him that kind of information access? Even if he'd been operating under an assumption or rumor, the possibility now under consideration was far too unorthodox for someone outside the sphere of IT&PA or Interpol intelligence to guess.

Somehow he had an inside source. Or maybe he had known he was up for the position two years ago.

And that whole business about Ledger having a thing for her had to be another guess. Ledger had never even looked at her beyond the standard greeting until about a year ago.

Drake couldn't know.

"The codes will arrive at the home of a certain businessman late tonight. They'll leave the country with him on Christmas Eve."

This time, she didn't stop walking. She absorbed his statements and considered the ramifications if he was correct. That would mean she still had time to get the copies she needed. Depending upon who the businessman was and whether or not she could get close to him in such a short time frame.

But she had no way of knowing if Drake was telling her the truth or not.

"His buyer is someone you know rather well."

She didn't slow down. She walked right on, choosing to stay on the outer boundaries of the vineyards. Anyone who might be home on the property would definitely notice people tromping through along their rows.

Not that she'd noticed anyone at home so far. Though the farmhouses were few and far between, you would think she would encounter at least one vineyard owner or worker. Where the hell was everybody?

Maybe they were all out Christmas shopping.

The little monologue going on inside her head didn't work as well as she'd hoped at keeping her mind off Drake's attempts at drawing her into conversation.

If IT&PA or Interpol knew the name of the buyer, then she would know. Drake was wrong. He was fishing again. Trolling for information.

"Ledger is playing both sides of the fence these days."

Now that got her attention.

No way could she let that remark pass.

"Ledger is not playing both sides of the fence."

Drake never had liked the guy. There had always been a fierce competition between them. An unhealthy need to outdo each other.

"He isn't going to get away with it, but I don't want you caught in the middle when he goes down. He'll try to use you, Sabrina."

"I can take care of myself, Drake."

The problem was, she just didn't see what he was up to. What was his agenda here? If he really knew who the buyer was, why wasn't he long gone?

There was no reason for him to hang around here with her. Especially considering she pretty much blamed him for her current predicament. If he hadn't forced her to the luggage compartment of that train, she'd be in Troyes by now with the information she needed to intercept the courier.

This whole mess was entirely his fault.

Except for the guy on the train who'd reveled in knowing he'd caught Sabrina Fox.

That was the one sticking point.

No, if she'd listened to Drake she wouldn't have ended up captured. He'd been right—at least about that part.

"He's setting you up to take the fall so that the whole screwup to come can be blamed on you."

A laugh burst out of her throat. "You mean the way you did two years ago?"

That kept him quiet for all of a minute.

"Two years ago was a mistake."

Okay, now he'd really piqued her interest. She stopped, grabbed him by the arm and forced him to face her. "So now you're admitting that you screwed me over? Is that right?"

"That's right."

The sincerity in those blue eyes tugged at her, made her want to believe whatever he said. But two years of bitterness wouldn't allow her to be so naive.

"You cheated on me, Drake." The fury behind those words made her want to kick herself. She hadn't wanted him to know, ever, how badly he'd hurt her. And yet she'd informed him repeatedly since he'd intruded into her current mission.

"I was wrong. The end doesn't always justify the means. I made a mistake. Maybe I was a little scared."

For two long years, she had hated him. Not once had she allowed herself to cry over the jerk. She'd been too angry, too determined not to let him touch her that way. But tears or no, he'd hurt her more than any man had ever hurt her before. No man had ever gotten to her the way Eric Drake had. She'd loved him, dammit.

Her hand fell away from his arm. She couldn't

bear to know that any part of her was connected to him. "I don't want to hear this."

"My superiors were convinced it was the only way. They were right. It was the only way. But I shouldn't have made the choice I did."

There it was—the bottom line.

"You chose the job over me."

She'd wanted to say those words to him for more than two years, but somehow saying them now didn't assuage the anger smoldering inside her. What was worse, she knew without doubt she would have done the same thing…wouldn't she?

"I did. I was wrong. I needed to prove to myself that I hadn't lost it, that I could still do whatever it took regardless of how I felt about you."

She suddenly yearned to reach out to him. To tell him not to worry about it, the whole thing was in the past now. No need to look back.

Thank God good sense kicked in before she did exactly that.

Fury decimated those more tender feelings.

"Damn straight you were wrong."

She did a right face and resumed the journey toward the village that somehow seemed to get farther away rather than closer.

He trailed after her. She didn't have to look back or hear him. She could feel him within arm's reach. She hated that she could still do that… feel him.

His silence lasted a little longer than the usual couple of minutes this time.

"I don't expect you to forgive me."

"Good thing." Because she didn't plan to.

"It would be nice if we could get past it and work together on this the way we did before."

She laughed again; this time, the sound came freely. "Dream on, Drake. We'll never do anything the way we did before."

"The fact that I probably saved your life back there doesn't matter?"

Another laugh rumbled up from her chest. "I wouldn't have needed you to save my life if you hadn't interfered with my mission. So that negates anything you did that may or may not have helped me out. Besides, you'd be dead right now if I hadn't distracted the guy who had you on your knees."

She didn't mention that it was the second time today she'd seen him in that position. Maybe the Dragon was losing his touch. No, that was a lie. He'd only ended up in that position because she had refused to listen to his warnings on the train.

"That's what happens when a guy lets a woman get under his skin. He loses focus. That's what had me scared to death two years ago."

Now there was a priceless comeback.

"There was a time when you didn't need excuses, Drake."

She'd expected him to retaliate with a cutting remark of his own, or at least a pithy comment that would put her in her place.

Instead he said, "That was before."

She absolutely refused to ask before what. He wanted her to do that. She wouldn't.

This was so not a part of the job.

Even when they had been deep into their physical relationship, they had never allowed personal feelings to interfere with a mission like this.

Not once.

She ignored the little voice that suggested that maybe fear of where their relationship was headed *had* interfered two years ago. That was giving him far too much credit. He didn't deserve it.

"I was just as startled by the change in my ability to put all else aside as you."

"Don't care. Don't care. Don't care," she chanted. It was the only way she'd ever been able to get her sister to shut up back when they were kids. Maybe it would work on Drake.

She wasn't so lucky.

"We'd been over about six months when it really hit me."

Don't care. Don't care. Don't care. She tried to block the words. To somehow prevent them from penetrating into the brain cells that would overanalyze what he may or may not have meant.

"I'd made a mistake. I'd hurt you. All because I was afraid of allowing you so much power over me."

She did not want to hear this.

"I'm not going to stop, you know. Not until you listen."

She walked faster.

He manacled her arm, hauled her around to face him.

"I'm not listening, Dra—"

His mouth came down on hers. He kissed her brutally. The tang of blood reminded her that he had an injured lip. She tried to push him away. Tried to ignore the sensations.

Impossible.

She relented.

Let the feel of his mouth against hers overwhelm all else. No man had ever kissed her the way Eric had. With his whole body and soul. He poured every ounce of his being into the kiss. And every part of her reacted.

She melted against him. Let her body mold to his. Trumpets sounded and angels sung. She was home. No place had ever felt as right as being in his arms.

If he'd had such a life-altering revelation about how he really felt, why had it taken him all this time to tell her? To apologize?

Because it was a trick.

She shoved at his broad chest again.

He kept kissing her…devouring her lips as if he were a starving man and she was the last possible feast on the planet.

She shoved harder, tried to turn her face away from his.

He drew back just far enough away to drag in a desperate breath. "I've missed you."

Again she tried to push him away. "Get off me."

He blinked, stared down at her as if he'd just snapped out of a trance.

"Back off, Drake!"

All the warm, fuzzy sensations his kiss had evoked were gone. Replaced by fiery anger.

"I couldn't help myself," he admitted without an iota of remorse in his tone or his eyes.

She tore out of his clutches. "Just see that it doesn't happen again."

He dropped his hands to his sides and took a step back. "It won't happen again."

"Good." She straightened her coat. "We need to keep moving. It'll be dark soon. I can't afford to waste any more time."

"Nor can I."

At least they were in agreement about something.

The question was, how long would any agreement they reached last?

Long enough to stay alive and get those codes?

CHAPTER TWELVE

DARKNESS HAD FALLEN by the time they reached the village. The reason they hadn't encountered any property owners along their way was because of a Christmas festival. Residents from the surrounding countryside were packed into the tiny village.

Thankfully there was still a room available at one of the inns. What was even more surprising was Drake's ingenuity with a new ID and cash.

"I have to admit," she confessed, "I wouldn't have thought to look there."

"That's the point." He gifted her with one of those wide, charming smiles that had stolen her heart soon after they met three years ago. No man should be able to wield that much power with only his lips.

He placed the insole back into his shoe and tugged it on. The pair of Nikes had been especially designed for him. A removable insole revealed a small compartment in which he carried a new ID and cash.

The ID, a French driver's license, identified him as Paul Dillion.

"I'll get the room. You wait here. I don't think it's a good idea for us to be seen together."

He was right. And it wasn't as if she could take off on him. She didn't even have cash for a phone call. She probably could pick a pocket or two, or even sweet-talk her way into some ready cash, but she was exhausted. She needed a hot bath and some sleep. She needed to think.

But first she had to contact Protocol.

Maybe the bath first. She couldn't do anything at the moment anyway.

"Once I'm at the desk," he said as he laced his sneaker, "go in and head up the stairs as if you're already a registered guest. Wait for me on the second floor."

"Gotcha."

He hesitated before going inside. There wasn't much light in the narrow alley where they stood, but she didn't miss the uncertainty in his eyes.

"Don't run out on me, Sabrina. We have more than this mission that we need to resolve."

How could a girl take off after a line like that?

She watched him walk away, some part of her drawn to the way he moved.

How had she lived these last two years without him?

She leaned her head against the brick wall

behind her. She had to be out of her mind. Maybe the contusion was really a concussion. Her gray matter was definitely scrambled.

He was a mistake. Her mistake. He was heartbreak. Her heartbreak.

Letting him wheedle his way back into her heart would be stupid.

Once he'd had time to arrive at the desk, she pushed away from the wall and strolled to the entrance of the inn. The quaint eighteenth-century architecture made her think of long weekends and slow, easy sex. Or maybe it was the lingering side effects of that damned kiss that had her thinking so skewed.

The clerk behind the counter was female and totally enthralled with Drake, her latest guest. The woman wouldn't have noticed a whole boatload of castaways sneaking up her staircase.

Sabrina didn't hang around to watch. She knew about Drake's charm firsthand. He was lethal. He should come with a warning label.

Upstairs she leaned against a window and watched the revelers outside. Christmas was scarcely three days away. The closer it came, the less likely she was to arrive in Kansas on time to celebrate with her family. She could feel the pull of disappointment already. This was one time she couldn't let her sister down.

She had to get her hands on those codes.

Soon.

And then she had to get the hell out of the country before she made the second major mistake of her life.

Her first major mistake bounded up the stairs and dangled a key at her. "Here we go."

The room was on the second floor at the south end of the inn. Drake unlocked the door and stepped aside for her to enter the room first.

A large four-poster bed decorated with satin and lace stood in the center of the room. An ornate fireplace prepped with wood for igniting gave the room a cozy feel, even without flickering flames. A wide set of windows looked out over the streets below. Very nice. Intensely romantic.

Sabrina crossed the room and checked the phone. A dial tone signaled direct access. Maybe she'd make that call now.

Since the table where the phone sat was near the door to the bathroom, she dragged the phone into the bathroom with her and closed the door.

When she'd started the water running in the massive claw-footed tub, she put through her call.

The automated voice of Protocol asked for her access number. She entered the number and recited her code phrase for the voice analysis.

Since she no longer had her cell phone, her location wouldn't be automatically provided. Passing along that information via a landline wouldn't be smart. Protocol would use the number she'd dialed from to triangulate her location. It would take longer, but the result would be the same. The voice came back with a simple statement.

"Your destination remains unchanged. No further instructions are required at this time."

That was good.

She replaced the receiver on the base and stood.

The fact that her orders were unchanged meant that the codes were still in the country. It also meant that there was still an opportunity to intercept the courier before final delivery.

Drake's allegations against Ledger intruded on her thoughts. If his goal was to have her eliminated, then he certainly wouldn't have shown up in New York attempting to woo her into a relationship. Admittedly, Drake didn't know that part. She didn't know what he hoped to gain by making such bold statements, but she wasn't putting any stock in anything Drake had to say.

Nor was she going to be swayed by his kisses or his apologies.

Whatever he was up to, he would only be using her just as he'd done before.

Then again…her apartment had been broken into and she had discovered someone following her…both while Ledger was in New York.

"Stop it," she muttered. Ledger was not her enemy. Drake was messing with her head.

Stripping off her clothes, she checked the available bath salts and scents and made her selection. She inhaled deeply of the steamy, scented water.

She could relax now. Her mission was still on target and she had a tub full of hot water calling her name. She stepped into the tub, moaned as the hot water swirled around her weary legs.

Her breath caught as she lowered her sore, aching body fully into the depths of pure liquid heat. God, it felt so good. Her nipples hardened with distinct pleasure. She refused to consider that the man in the next room might have a hand in that. No way. This was about another kind of heavenly pleasure. A long, hot soak after a grueling day.

She totally lost track of time. It felt so damned good to soak in the water. Her mind wandered to last Friday night and the numerous moments of ecstasy she'd reached with…what's his name. Oh, yeah. David. How could she have forgotten his name? She thought of all the ways he'd brought her to climax. The wicked images filtered one after the other through her mind.

Her breath caught sharply when she realized that she'd superimposed Drake's face over David's. She sat up, realized the water had grown cold, and cursed herself for being a total idiot.

She drained the tub partially and turned the water back on to wash her hair with the tiny bottles of complimentary shampoo and conditioner. Careful of the tender spot on her head, she massaged her scalp and forced herself to relax once more. When she'd thoroughly rinsed her hair for the last time, she finished draining the tub. She rinsed away the last of the bubbles, then draped herself in a big, fluffy towel.

She thoroughly rinsed her panties in the sink since she'd have no choice but to wear them again tomorrow and placed them on the window ledge above the oil radiator to dry.

After scrutinizing her reflection in the mirror she decided she needed a comb or brush, but neither of those was provided. She remembered that Drake had a comb in his hip pocket. Maybe she'd borrow it.

She opened the door to the bedroom to find the room lit by nothing but candles and the roaring flames from the logs in the fireplace. The idea of how much heat would emanate from that fire drew her in that direction.

"Room service just brought up dinner." Drake gestured to the cart. "Start without me."

He disappeared into the bathroom. She forgot all about the comb and the fire. The smells emoting from the room service cart were too wonderful to ignore. Her stomach rumbled greedily.

She filled a plate with succulent meats and sautéed vegetables. She didn't even bother with a fork since it felt too good bringing the delicious food to her lips with her bare fingers. After pouring a flute of champagne, she took her food to the bed and climbed on. She didn't care if Drake heard her sounds of satisfaction. The food was just too good not to make sounds.

The champagne was the best she'd ever had. Of course they were in champagne country.

When she'd devoured everything on her plate, she went back in search of more. Strawberries dipped in chocolate. A light, airy cake that didn't need frosting. More champagne. If she'd ever eaten anything this good, she couldn't recall it. Maybe because she hadn't eaten since the couple of bites she'd had at the hotel restaurant that morning with Segelman. Or maybe just because she needed to be sated by something besides the presence of Eric Drake.

Who hadn't substituted food for sex at least once?

Whatever the case, she ate until she was stuffed. Then she drank some more.

She'd almost fallen asleep against the mound of pillows when she heard the bathroom door open. She sat up, adjusted her towel and took her empty plate back to the cart.

"There's a second robe if you'd like one."

It wasn't until he spoke that she looked at him. He wore a white robe. His broad shoulders tested the size and the belt cinched around his lean waist making the vee shape impossible to ignore. His coal-black hair was still damp, and his face was clean shaven. She hadn't noticed shaving accoutrements. Where the hell had he gotten a razor? Did he have deodorant in there, as well?

He rubbed his chin, as if reading her mind. "Room service. They provided toothbrushes and deodorant, as well."

Sure enough, right there on the table next to the bed were two toothbrushes and toothpaste and a brand of roll-on that she didn't recognize.

She snatched a toothbrush, the deodorant and the toothpaste and returned to the bathroom. She should have thanked him, but she couldn't muster the necessary humility.

When she'd brushed her teeth, she rounded up the other robe and pulled it on in place of the towel. She'd hoped that her loitering in the bathroom had ensured that she missed having to watch Drake eat.

Apparently her luck had taken a turn for the worse the moment he stormed back into her life.

He'd just poured himself a glass of champagne. He lifted the bottle as if to salute her reappearance. "More?"

She shook her head. She'd already had too much. The warm, fuzzy feeling had cloaked her far too thoroughly.

Fiddling with the covers for a bit, she drew

back the coverlet, tossed aside the decorative pillows, then climbed onto the bed. She didn't ask where he intended to sleep. Since he had room service at his beck and call, he could surely have them conjure up a rollaway.

When he started making those sensuous sounds related to the incredible food and his, no doubt, ravenous appetite, she closed her eyes and tried to block the nerve-jangling noise.

It didn't help.

As tightly as she squeezed her eyes shut she couldn't keep them closed. She had to see. Had to watch his lips and tongue relish the food. Like her, he used his fingers. Long, blunt-tipped fingers that made her think of all the places on her body he'd explored with them. His tongue flicked out and licked those fingers, and she shivered. Images of that wicked tongue slipping over her skin, delving into damp places made her muscles contract with delicious need. Her nipples stood at attention once more, and this time she couldn't blame the reaction on anything but him.

He selected a strawberry naked of chocolate and dipped it into his glass. He sank his teeth into the plump red flesh and champagne trickled down his chin.

A moan ripped past her lips before she could stop it.

His gaze locked with hers and she started to cough.

She sat up, tugged the covers up around her as she coughed frantically in an attempt to cover for her temporary lapse into moral depravity.

"Here."

She glanced up, unable to meet his eyes, before accepting the glass of water. "Thank you," she mumbled hoarsely.

She sipped the water, coughed a little more just to be sure he bought her cover.

He, damn him, sat right back down in front of that flickering fire and took up right where he'd left off. This time he licked the chocolate on the strawberry, suckled it like a nipple before taking a leisurely bite. Her pulse reacted instantly. Her body heated as if she were the one sitting so close to the fire...as if he'd nibbled on her like that.

The heat he sat so near had encouraged a flush on his skin. He closed his eyes and relished his food as if it might be his last meal. Watching him made her so aroused she could scarcely lie still. Her fingers were knotted in the sheet. How could the mere act of eating be so incredibly sexy? Unbelievably her body was poised on the brink of a climax and he hadn't even touched her.

"That was amazing." He stood after he finished eating, stretched that lean body and then stalked over to the cart to deposit his empty plate there. "Would you like anything else?"

She managed a side-to-side motion of her head. No way would she attempt to speak.

"Good night." She pulled the covers up to her neck and closed her eyes. The sooner she went to sleep, the sooner this night would be over.

She held her breath, afraid that at any second she would feel the mattress shift beneath his weight. That would simply be more than she could take.

She was a tough secret agent, but she had her limits. Her body was already primed and humming after watching him eat. No way could she tolerate lying in this bed next to him. She could only hope he'd get the message and make other arrangements.

Unless she invited him, he wouldn't dare just climb in. Would he?

When the seconds turned into minutes and he didn't attempt to join her, she finally relaxed.

The distant sound of holiday music and the occasional cheer from the lingering crowd outside helped to lull her to sleep. She didn't remember letting go…but it happened just the same.

THE SOUND OF RIPPING fabric rasped across her senses. She tried to ignore it…but the sound came again and she had to open her eyes.

Darkness had invaded the room. The fire had died

and the only light was a narrow wedge that seeped past the crack left in the doorway to the bathroom.

A groan split the silence.

Not the pleasurable kind like when she'd been in the tub or devouring her dinner. No. This one was about pain and discomfort.

Sabrina threw back the covers and dropped her feet to the cold wood floor.

Another groan and a little grunting.

What the hell was Drake doing in there?

She got up and padded silently to the door. For about ten seconds she listened and heard more ripping, more groaning and the occasional sigh of frustration.

Hoping the door wouldn't creak, she pushed it inward.

Drake, naked except for his boxer briefs, stood in front of the mirror attempting to tie what was left of a sheet or pillowcase around his midsection.

"What're you doing?"

He twisted toward her and grimaced.

"Why didn't you say you were hurt?" She entered the bathroom and walked straight over to him. He was attempting to wrap his ribs with a ripped-up sheet or pillowcase.

"I didn't want you to worry."

Judging by the sweat beaded on his brow, he'd been at this for a while.

"That's just dumb, Drake." She scrutinized his handiwork. "It's still not tight enough."

He heaved a disgusted breath. "Not nearly tight enough."

She shook her head and let go her own frustrated sigh. "You know what you need is a doctor. Cracked ribs are not something you ignore."

His intense blue gaze bored into hers. "Are you going to assist me, Agent Fox, or are you going to lecture me?"

Men. They refused to ask for directions when they were lost and they hated seeking medical attention when they were injured. Dumb.

She untied his untidy knots and loosened the makeshift bandage. He kept his arms folded over the top of his head.

"How long have you been in here?" It was past midnight. She'd slept like the dead for several hours. Surely he hadn't been working on this all that time.

"I tried to sleep for a while."

Her eyebrows raised in question.

"In the chair," he clarified.

"That couldn't have been comfortable." She almost felt guilty. *Almost*.

"Tell me about it."

What she really needed was pins if there was any chance of getting this makeshift bandage tight enough. "Do you think your little friend from the front desk would mind getting a call at this time of night?"

"Pins?" he guessed.

She nodded.

"Maybe with your help," he suggested, obviously not wanting any other females to know his weaknesses, "I can hold this end while you pull it tight."

"Fine. Whatever." She wasn't going to argue with him. If he wanted to be in pain, that was his problem.

She smoothed one end of the makeshift bandage around his middle between his belly button and his pecs. "Okay, hold it right there while I pull."

He held the end in place while she pulled the fabric around his ribs. When she'd reached his hands, she held the fabric in place while he tied the necessary knots. He'd done a nice job of creating small tails to tie together. She wasn't completely confident that it would work, but it very well could hold.

"Getting any support?" She surveyed her handiwork. She had her doubts but if it made him happy, who was she to complain?

"Better."

As if her senses had been set on delay she abruptly felt the need to shiver with the remembered feel of his skin as she'd tugged that fabric around him. Hot, smooth. Like silk stretched over steel.

He stood several inches taller than her. His shoulders were inordinately wide, especially when he was shirtless as he was now. They seemed to go on forever. The width tapered into a lean waist and narrow hips. Long, muscular legs attested to the fact that he still ran every day. When they'd been together, his routine had been to run five miles per day. She didn't know about now. She didn't want to know.

Her gaze moved back up to his face. His cheek was discolored just a little, not much. The lip didn't look so bad; it was only slightly swollen in one corner.

She felt him watching her a full three seconds before her gaze bumped into his. Feeling suddenly naked, she pulled the lapels of the robe more snugly around her and squared her shoulders against her own irritating vulnerability.

"You need aspirin or something for the pain?" She hated that her voice sounded so deep and thick. Maybe he'd chalk it up to the idea that she'd only just awakened from a deep sleep.

"Not necessary."

The tension between them heightened to the point where it was difficult for her to breathe.

"Well, good night, then."

She'd almost gotten away.

He curled the fingers of one hand around her wrist and tugged her back around to face him.

For far too many seconds, he simply stared into her eyes. She told herself to look away, but her body refused to obey.

"Thank you."

The whispered words brushed across her senses. Made her think of long, hot nights filled with sweaty sex and long, soothing baths. With him.

She had to get out of here.

"You're…ah…welcome."

She backed up a step. He released her arm, his gaze never leaving hers. Before she could change her mind, she turned around and walked across the cold bathroom tiles. She didn't stop until she'd climbed back into bed and pulled the covers up close around her.

Sleep, she ordered, shutting her eyes closed.

Ignore him.

Don't talk to him.

Don't open your eyes.

She heard the soft sound of his bare feet as he moved across the room to settle in the chair. The even softer sound of discomfort that whispered across his lips made her body react as if she'd felt the pain.

This was ridiculous. They were both adults. Adults who had shared every imaginable intimacy. They could certainly share the same bed for a few hours.

Disgusted with herself, she opened her eyes and blinked until they adjusted to the near darkness. Lying here pretending that his discomfort didn't matter was just stupid. They both needed sleep.

"There's plenty of room over here," she said, her voice quavering in spite of her every effort to sound strong and firm.

"I'll be fine here."

She should leave it at that. But her foolish nurturing instinct wouldn't let her.

"Don't be ridiculous, Drake. Come to bed. You'll never sleep in that chair."

The creak of the chair signaled he'd gotten up. She froze, not even daring to look in his direction as she imagined him crossing the room. She felt the subtle shift of the mattress as he climbed beneath the covers and settled.

"Just stay on your side," she warned.

"Don't worry." He laid back with a muffled groan and pulled the covers up. "I'm in no condition to give you any trouble tonight."

Maybe he could fool himself with that tortured statement but she knew better. All she would have to do is roll over and give him the slightest provocation and he'd forget all about any pain he felt. She knew him too well. That was the primary reason why what she'd just allowed was so incredibly shortsighted.

"I know you don't trust me, Sabrina," he said

out of the blue. "But I need you to set aside our past differences until this is over. It's the only way we'll get through it."

Lying there in the dark with the deep, husky sound of his voice resonating around her, it would be so easy to believe him. To pretend the past had never happened and just go with the moment.

But she knew better than to trust him or herself where he was concerned.

He'd betrayed her once. And they'd been sleeping together. They hadn't seen each other in two years. There was absolutely nothing that bound them now, not even the past. How could she possibly trust that he wouldn't let her down again?

She couldn't.

It was that simple.

And vastly complicated at the same time.

"I can't promise you anything right now, Drake," she confessed, deciding that she needed to be up front with him. "The mission is top priority. As long as you don't get in my way, we won't have a problem."

That seemed straightforward and fair enough, in her opinion. If they were going to be stuck together in this situation for a while longer, it only made sense to be up front with each other.

From her perspective, at least, it made sense. Maybe he had other ideas. He wouldn't be regaining her trust without a definite show of faith.

For several seconds, she thought he wasn't going to respond. But then he did.

"That being the case, then I must warn you we already have a problem."

CHAPTER THIRTEEN

SABRINA WOKE TO the sun pouring in through the windows on the other side of the room.

It couldn't be past seven. She never slept past seven.

She took a moment to get her bearings.

France.

Inn.

Drake.

She froze.

He was in bed with her.

Not only had she just remembered that fact, but she could now feel the heat from his body where he lay nestled against her back.

Her senses kicked into high gear.

Oh, damn.

If she moved, unbearable friction would result. She knew this because his aroused anatomy was pressed firmly against her bottom.

One heavily muscled arm lay across her waist. The other...

She stilled.

The other was looped beneath her, the palm of that hand flat against her belly.

She had to move.

No way she could continue to lie here like this.

The best option was to make a swift break. No hesitation. Just move.

She took a breath and propelled herself upward using her elbow.

The arm tightened around her waist and pulled her back against Drake's masculine body.

Now, the arm lying on top of her curled against her. The accompanying hand cupped her breast.

Desire roared through her. She bit her fist to hold back a cry of need. It took every ounce of control she possessed not to wiggle her buttocks against his arousal.

His face burrowed into her hair, his lips pressed against her neck. Shivers scattered across her skin. His hand squeezed her breast and she barely restrained the urge to twist around and…

The pad of his thumb brushed across her nipple.

She considered elbowing him to wake him up and hopefully avoid any embarrassment since she could pretend to still be asleep. But she couldn't risk doing any additional damage to his ribs.

Even if he did deserve the bonus pain.

For another minute or so she lay there, undecided as to what she should do next. At some point, she considered that she'd never known him to be such a heavy sleeper. Surely he'd wake up any second now.

Maybe he was awake.

Maybe he was enjoying every minute of this.

"Drake!"

His face nuzzled her neck. "Hmmm."

"Get off me!"

She shoved at his arm.

He tensed. She felt the contraction of his muscles as if it had been her body seizing.

Then there was this little gasp.

"Get off me," she repeated.

"Yeah…okay."

She didn't know how he managed the feat, but he rolled away from her without groaning in pain. He rushed into the bathroom and shut the door so fast she scarcely got a glimpse of movement.

Rolling onto her back, she stared at the ceiling. Her body vibrated like a tuning fork. Need coursed through her veins. She closed her eyes and thought of all those orgasms she'd had only a few days ago, and she had to admit that not a single one of them had pushed her this close to the edge of utter implosion.

This need was so ruthless it was almost painful.

The sound of water in the bathroom's sink had her listening intently. Was he in there struggling with the same need she was?

She closed her eyes and tried to force her body back into submission.

It didn't work.

Instead she imagined him coming down on top of her...sliding that hardened part of him inside her. Slow, easy strokes. Her hips started to rock as memories of all the times they'd made love flashed across the private theatre of her mind. Before she could grab back control, the waves of completion were taking her the full distance.

It felt so good.

Too damned good.

Sabrina threw back the covers and got up just as the bathroom door opened. He'd pulled on his jeans but he'd failed to completely fasten the fly. Her gaze went straight to that pivotal juncture.

She swallowed hard...wondered if he'd just...

"Good morning."

His voice sounded totally nonchalant...as if nothing had happened...as if she hadn't just climaxed thinking about him. Fury obliterated all those soft, warm feelings. Her gaze flew up to his face. And right there was all the proof she'd needed that he wasn't nearly so unaffected as he'd like her to believe. The fire in his eyes told her he was still thinking about how it had felt to be nestled so snugly behind her. She moistened her lips and tried not to let the fire rekindle.

"Good morning."

They passed only inches apart, him exiting the bathroom, her entering.

Her body shuddered sweetly at his nearness even for that instant.

Somehow she had to shake this off. She washed her face. Stared at her reflection and told herself what a fool she was.

This was the man who'd betrayed her and then walked away without explanation. She'd tried to contact him, but he'd vanished. No one knew what the hell had happened to him. Then self-preservation had kicked in and she'd refused to even wonder, at least out loud.

She shouldn't feel anything for him. Least of all unbridled desire.

Her panties were dry. She frowned as she studied their positioning on the window ledge. She'd spread them out so they would dry more quickly. They lay pretty much crumpled into a wad now.

Comprehension dawned.

He'd touched her panties.

"You are a wicked boy," she murmured.

When she'd wiggled into her panties, she rounded up the rest of her clothes and got dressed. Before exiting the bathroom she brushed her teeth and used the comb she found on the sink. She was pretty sure it belonged to Drake. He'd probably left it there for her. With the mass of blond tangles flying around her head, she could see why he might think to do that.

By the time she'd tamed her locks, the smell of fresh brewed coffee had filtered past the closed door. Her stomach grumbled impatiently. She was starved. A good climax, like a challenging battle, always left her ravenous.

In the other room, Drake had poured two cups of coffee and was embellishing a croissant with fruit spread. He set his pastry aside and offered her a cup of the steaming coffee.

"Thank you." She took the cup, careful that her fingers didn't brush his.

They ate in silence. The fruit and pastries were heavenly.

As she finished her third cup of coffee, she decided it was time to end this tenuous relationship.

"I need to be on my way this morning, Drake." She placed her cup carefully on the tray. "I hope you'll understand when I say that this is something I need to finish alone. We're not on the same team anymore, and we're bound to get in each other's way."

He set his own cup aside. "As I told you last night, I don't intend to let you out of my sight."

She caught herself staring at his lips as he spoke. She had to stop that. This whole situation had gotten completely out of control.

"I don't get your angle, Drake, but this is not going to work."

He took a step in her direction. "There is no angle. My only concern is you."

Oh, now that was good. He'd gotten her all hot and bothered and now he was going for the final tackle—her disintegrating intellect.

"You said you were after the same thing I was, remember?" He had to remember. He'd said those very words to her on the train just yesterday.

"Isn't your goal to complete your mission without getting yourself killed?"

How the hell did he know to say that?

Sure, it was every agent's goal to complete her mission without getting herself killed. But the idea that Marx had said those very words to her…that Drake stood here and echoed them now was just too much of a coincidence.

"My mission is to protect you." He lifted those broad shoulders of his and let them fall. "So, we're essentially after the same thing."

Part of her wanted to trust him. Probably the stupid part that still thought about the brick ranch-style house her sister owned and her two kids and the dog. But the more rational, savvy New York woman side of her was suspicious.

"All right, Drake, you win." She closed the distance between them now, one step, then another. "You stick with me while I get this done. Watch my back. Whatever. But if you get in my way, I swear I'll kill you."

That was a promise.

"Deal."

THE WINTER SKY LOOKED like blue glass. The sun was still low, the wind sharp as a knife.

Drake slowed as they approached Troyes, an old city with timbered buildings and dozens of cafés with Portuguese names. Signs of Christmas were everywhere, reminding her of how little time she had left to finish this mission and get back to the States.

Sabrina allowed herself a moment to appreciate the medieval architecture that had stood since before Attila the Hun. The ancient capital town of Champagne on the Seine, east-southeast of Paris, stood to this day, filled with churches, basilicas and history.

The narrow jumble of streets and alleyways were designed for walking, Sabrina thought. Many of the passageways were far too narrow for a car, even one as small as the one they had.

They parked the car Drake had rented and joined the crowd of pedestrians touring the Christmas market or watching the ice sculptors while simultaneously standing in line for the little train ride to the carousel.

The whole scene was so normal. So everyday.

That she was here for a mission felt entirely wrong, somehow.

Annoyance flamed deep in her belly.

This was why she should stay away from Drake. He made her feel like this. This whole longing for normalcy. Her life was not normal. It would never be normal.

The idea that her mentor was retiring from this life made her want to take a break and reflect on all that she sacrificed to lead this abnormal life.

Life was changing all around her. She just wanted to stay the same…status quo. Uncomplicated.

Why did that suddenly have to be so hard?

"What's your rendezvous point?"

She snapped back to the here and now.

What the hell was wrong with her?

She needed a phone.

"I'll let you know when the time comes," she said to him. If he just hadn't bulldozed his way back into her life, she wouldn't be feeling like this now.

Damn him.

When she'd located a throng of tourists, she followed them until she saw what she needed.

An American tourist with a cell phone clipped to his belt. Had to be an international phone or he wouldn't be carrying it so handy.

She moved into the group, made sure she was in position for full body contact and then made her move. She slammed into him.

"Excusez-moi."

She went off on a tangent in French. He stared at her bewildered and more than a little annoyed.

When he waved her off and walked away, she pivoted and headed away from the crowd, his phone in her hand.

She found a quiet corner in the shadow of a towering building constructed mainly of timbers and entered Protocol's number. After she'd gone through the ID process, she said, "Destination accomplished."

She waited while that information processed, then she mentally noted the address of her rendez-vous point and the name she should use.

After severing the connection, she deleted the call from the phone's recent calls directory. She scanned the recently dialed calls and selected the only one that was a local Troyes number. The call was answered after two rings. The name of a hotel was announced, and Sabrina closed the phone. Now she knew where the tourist was staying. She would drop his phone by the desk of his hotel.

The *hôtel de ville* was her rendezvous point.

She grabbed a local map and took a moment to locate it as well as the hotel where the American tourist was staying.

For the most part, she ignored Drake.

The cobblestoned alley she took was like the rest. The timber buildings seemed to lean into one another. Any other time she would have liked to have explored more of the rustic village with the Seine coiled around it. But there wasn't time.

The men who'd attempted to stop her yesterday would not give up so easily.

Though she was reasonably sure they hadn't been followed to this point, she couldn't be certain.

And in this business, anything less than certainty was unacceptable.

She dropped the tourist's phone off at the desk of his hotel before moving on to her destination. Drake didn't ask any questions. He stayed in her shadow and that, frankly, surprised her.

At the *hôtel de ville* she didn't enter immediately. Taking stock of the situation was necessary for a number of reasons.

The biggest reason was this thing with Drake. And the idea that the guy on the train had known her and her reputation.

Something was off.

She wasn't even going to throw Drake's accusations against Ledger into the mix.

Sabrina had learned long ago from the Director, Marx that, when something was off, a good agent stepped back and took stock of the circumstances.

"You're beginning to feel it."

Drake's comment shouldn't have irritated her but it did. She didn't need or want his opinion. There was a very good chance that her sudden trepidation was entirely his doing.

"Shut up, Drake. I don't need your input."

"Sabrina."

He touched her arm and she wanted to scream. Why did he have to show up in her life now and make her feel all these things she shouldn't feel?

"Back off or our deal is done."

He withdrew his hand and kept his mouth shut.

She tried not to enjoy the rush of power too much, but she couldn't help herself. She liked being able to control the man who could have her so riddled with desire with just his presence. Turnabout was fair play, after all. Then again, she'd had him pretty much out of sorts this morning, as well.

"I'll be back. Order some coffee or something." She left Drake beneath the canopy of a small café and walked casually across the street.

Inside the hotel the lobby was quiet; only one guest waited. He flipped through a newspaper. Maybe he was waiting for his wife who was still upstairs in the room. A cigarette dangled from his lips. The wife probably didn't like him to smoke in their room, so he had no choice but to come down to the lobby.

Keeping him in her peripheral vision, she strode up to the desk. "Good morning. My name is Carreau. I believe you have a message for me."

The clerk considered her a long moment, most likely verifying the physical description he'd been given. "Yes, madame." He reached beneath the counter and retrieved a nine-by-twelve manila envelope. He smiled broadly as he presented it to her.

She thanked him. A tip wasn't necessary. The contact who'd left it would have taken care of that part of the exchange.

As she turned to go, the man with the newspaper stood. Tension roiled through her.

A flash of mink and stilettos rushed into her line of vision from the opposite direction. The wife, she realized. The woman was already issuing orders before she reached her waiting husband. The two scurried through the exit without a backward glance. The relief played havoc with Sabrina's knees. Man, she was really off-kilter on this one.

She had to regain her perspective. She couldn't keep letting her emotions rule her.

Her determination solidified, she strolled back out onto the street. She surveyed the clutches of tourists and then zeroed in on Drake across the street. He'd taken a table and ordered two cups of coffee, as well as a plate of bread.

When she reached the table, he stood.

"I assume all went well." He glanced pointedly at the envelope.

"So it would seem." She settled into the chair across from him and he resumed his own.

The sweet bread looked delicious, but she had no appetite.

She did, however, indulge her need for more caffeine.

After breaking the seal on the envelope, she reached inside and removed the enclosed PDA. She turned it on and waited for all systems to fire up. Once the log-in page appeared, she entered the necessary ID and password. That step took her into the system. A quick swipe of her thumb across the biometrics pad and she moved to the next level.

The image of her target appeared. An older man, perhaps sixty. Gray hair and eyes. Attractive and distinguished. A profile was next, and then the stats on his current residence. He lived on an estate only a couple of hours from her current location.

The codes had been delivered to him this morning.

He would pass them off to his contact tonight at a grand gala in honor of a number of Paris's most elite citizens.

Since the original simple encounter with the courier had not gone down as planned, her team had been assembled at a rendezvous point a few miles from her target's residence. She could just imagine what Trainer thought of that last-minute arrangement. He preferred at least forty-eight hours' notice before traveling halfway around the world.

He rarely got what he wanted, and he never

failed to be ready or to complain. Sabrina was pretty sure he just liked the extra attention.

Sabrina took one last look at her target and then entered the data destruct code.

The display flickered and then went black. All data stored on the PDA was now inaccessible.

She reached into the envelope and pulled out the new secure cell phone and tucked it into the pocket of her coat.

"How much time do we have?"

She glanced up at Drake. "A couple of hours."

There was no need to rush.

In fact she wanted some time to see what she could get out of Drake. There was something about the way this whole scenario was playing out that felt wrong. Very wrong.

Somehow he was at the center of the problem. And, whether she wanted to lend credence to his accusations or not, she needed to determine why he'd suggested Ledger was working for the enemy.

Until two years ago, she and Drake had been as close as two humans could be. He'd been the best that Interpol had to offer and she'd been at the top of the heap from the U.S. side of the pond.

Their lives had meshed perfectly. They both had loved their work. Dedication and determination were the standards they had lived by.

The personal side of the relationship had felt right, as well.

She'd thought that he loved her.

But she'd been wrong.

Could she have been wrong about everything else, as well?

He'd dropped off her radar completely after that last joint mission. He'd disappeared.

Why?

What did he do now?

Why hadn't Ledger ever mentioned Drake? He was, after all, one of the Interpol's legends. She decided that Ledger's need to stay away from the topic of Drake was because he wanted to pursue a relationship with her. But she couldn't be sure. Perhaps Ledger hadn't mentioned him because he'd known how humiliated Sabrina had been by his betrayal.

Everyone knew.

Trainer, Hugh, Angie. And Marx.

Maybe that was why no one had ever talked about him or asked what happened to him. Even Marx had kept quiet on the subject. Had her friends been protecting her? They had all known that when Drake vanished, he'd walked out on her.

The burn of that old humiliation simmered inside her now. Despite the sting of that old betrayal, Drake still possessed the power to make her want him.

That was the part that galled her the most.

She wanted to deny she felt anything for him any longer. But that would be a lie. There was no denying it now.

No matter that he'd slept with another woman to accomplish his mission. No matter that he'd tromped on her heart to do it. She still wanted him.

Even now, sitting in this tiny café, she could feel his pull clear across the table.

He had taken some part of her with him when they'd walked away from each other two years ago. He hadn't apologized for his actions. He hadn't tried to make amends. He'd simply walked away. She had, too, but he'd taken the first step.

Now, after all this time, he had the nerve to show up and say he was sorry…that he'd made a mistake.

Oh, yeah, she wanted some time with him, all right.

She wanted to make him pay for every minute she had missed him. For every tear she had wanted to cry.

She wanted him to know the true meaning of devastation.

If there was any truth whatsoever to his apology and his admission that he'd made a mistake, maybe, just maybe, there was hope that she could hurt him the way he'd hurt her.

Maybe after the mission, she'd just tell him that the only thing he needed to worry about where

Ledger was concerned was whether she would end up with him. Considering the two had always been fiercely competitive, she was sure that would be a nice, low blow.

It wasn't exactly the most honorable thing she'd ever done, but the way she saw it, as long as she accomplished her mission, what did it matter?

Fire burned in her belly, this one fueled not by lust but the raging desire for revenge.

"We have a command performance tonight," she announced, setting the ball in motion.

"We?" Those blue eyes scrutinized her, suspicion already taking root.

"Yes, we. The codes have already been delivered. Our middle man plans to pass them off tonight at a grand function at his home. We're on his guest list." Actually *they* weren't on the guest list. She was. But then no one would be surprised when she brought an escort. It was expected.

A familiar glint of anticipation lit his eyes. "Need I ask what sort of function?"

"A costume ball." She set the now useless PDA aside. "I'm certain you'll fit in perfectly since you've always been such a master of deception."

She let him ponder that statement.

He wouldn't argue. He wanted in on this mission.

To protect her, he claimed.

But she wasn't convinced of that noble motivation.

He was Eric Drake the Dragon.

Everybody knew you couldn't trust a dragon to refrain from tossing out those devouring flames.

Drake had earned that name by consistently destroying his enemy. No one he targeted had ever escaped.

She should know.

She'd been burned by him before.

CHAPTER FOURTEEN

"WHAT WE HAVE here is your typical evening at the Phantom of the Opera gala attire."

Sabrina smiled at Angie's little flourish and wink. She knew the extra pep in Angie's presentation was for Drake, but that was okay. Angie was only human and Drake, well, he was pretty devastating.

Even Hugh was impressed. Maybe a little too much so.

Trainer was skeptical, but then he was always that way when another handsome male horned in on what he considered his territory.

The team knew Drake's reputation. Had even met him once or twice. But they had never worked on a mission with him.

In the past when Sabrina had worked a joint mission with Drake, Interpol had been lead.

This time, everything was different.

Including her.

No one outside this room could know Drake was on-site. Not even Marx. When Drake entered the house with Sabrina, he would be in disguise. Anyone monitoring the audio or visual of the mission would no doubt be accustomed to Sabrina's improvising so they wouldn't flinch.

That was the one point Drake insisted on, neither Interpol nor Marx could know he was involved.

The whole situation went against standard operating procedure, but instinct told her it was the right thing to do. She had to be out of her mind to trust Drake, or maybe some self-destructive gene just couldn't let the opportunity to get hurt again pass. Whatever the case, she'd made the decision. Right or wrong. Her team stood behind her. She hoped for their sakes that she wasn't making a mistake.

If Drake was using her to get his hands on the codes, she wanted to be the one to bring him down. At least that was what she told herself.

"The gown is an exact replica of the one worn in the theatre version of the play," Angie went on. "So is the tuxedo."

"They're gorgeous." Sabrina fingered the delicate material of the lovely gown.

"Communications is built in," Hugh said, stepping forward and taking the stage from Angie. He pointed to the gown's intricate bodice. "We've arranged for four members of Control to step in as waiters. All four will be heavily armed in the event they're needed."

Sabrina resisted the urge to frown. Control generally stood by off-site. That they would be on the scene surprised her. With Drake in the room, she wasn't going to question the decision.

"I'll be your operations coordinator tonight," Trainer said, cutting into the conversation.

Another surprise. "What will you be doing?" she asked Hugh.

He grinned widely. "I'm Angie's escort."

Okay, now she was really confused.

"Marx wants the two of us on-site," Angie explained.

Sabrina nodded, confusion cluttering her head. "Excellent. The more, the merrier."

"I'm Prince Charles and she's Camilla."

Now that picture would be worth the trouble of getting gussied up. "What about you, Trainer? Are you the only one without a costume?"

"I don't do costumes, Fox."

"Too cool, huh?"

"Someone has to do the real work," he said with a pointed look in her direction.

"Absolutely, I agree." The operation coordinator was not the guy to piss off.

"What about a digital camera?" she asked Hugh.

He held up a finger to indicate she should wait one second. From the look of glee on his face, this camera must be even better than the last.

The jeweled comb he held out in the palm of his hand was magnificent. "If you drop it or lose it afterwards, it won't matter. This one transmits directly to our system. Trainer will be able to pick it up on the monitor in the van stationed half a mile away."

"Cool." She picked up the comb, studied its design. Gorgeous.

She placed it next to her gown and stole a look in Drake's direction. That he'd kept quiet all this time seemed strange to her. He hadn't asked any questions. Hadn't made any suggestions.

Very strange.

"And this," Hugh said, dragging her back to the moment, "is your typical poison ring."

Sabrina studied the lovely ring with its massive stone.

"One little nudge here and it opens." He demonstrated. The stone popped up to reveal a small area where most anything in a tiny quantity could be packed. "Of course tonight there will be something inside. Dump it in your target's drink and he'll go beddy-bye for the whole night."

According to the profile, her target had a thing for younger women. She intended to prey upon that trait to gain access to what she needed. According to what IT&PA had ascertained regarding the residence, the safe was in the master bedroom suite. All she had to do was get in the room and give her target the drug.

"One last item," Hugh noted as he handed her what looked like a wide gold bracelet with a diamond-studded watch face. The decorative kind that looked glamorous and provided some practical use. "This is what you'll need to open the safe."

She checked out the watch. With a twist of the tiny stem used for setting the time, a digital display appeared. "Looks like you've got everything covered."

"As always," Hugh replied.

As if he'd only just awakened from a coma, Drake spoke up. His comment wasn't what she'd expected.

"All appears to be under control." He surveyed the group. "I'll be in my room if anyone needs me."

Then he left.

The house was a two-story, located less than five miles from the target residence. The grounds were crawling with control personnel. It wasn't as if she were worried that he'd take off on her at this point. It was more about his reactions being out of sync, somehow.

"So that's the legendary Dragon," Trainer noted. "I thought he'd be taller."

"He's taller than you as it is," Angie chided. "Handsome, too."

That last part she directed at Sabrina.

"Too bad he's straight," Hugh said wistfully.

As if they'd all remembered at the same instant that he was also the man who'd broken her heart, they started backpedaling.

"Well," Hugh revised, "if you like that type."

"Maybe he's too tall," Trainer amended.

"And stuck-up," Angie offered with a sniff.

"Gee." Sabrina looked from one to the other. "If I'd known what a jerk he was, I would never have gotten involved with him. Imagine."

Her friends looked at each other then, uncertain what to say.

"It's okay." She let them off the hook. "Every girl gets taken in by charm and good looks at some point in her life."

"How did he get involved in all this?"

Sabrina considered Trainer's question. She wasn't sure she could answer it. "I don't know exactly. He showed up on the train with a warning that I had been targeted."

"Marx didn't indicate anything like that when he briefed us," Angie said.

"I know." Sabrina knew without question that Marx would have let her know if he'd had intelligence to back up Drake's assertion.

"I get the impression that his participation is somewhat of a necessary evil."

Hugh nailed it.

"That's pretty much the way it is," Sabrina confessed. "If he's on the up and up, then I need him. If he's here to try and nab the codes, well…we all know what we have to do."

"We'll be watching your back," Angie assured her.

"We will," Hugh reiterated.

"Thanks, guys." She wasn't sure she knew how to put what she felt into words, but she had to try. "Somehow, this feels bigger than me." She considered her friends once more. "Do you know what I mean? It involves me on some level, but if it were merely about me, how come I'm not dead already?"

"Something is seriously off on this whole mission," Trainer said. "Even Marx acted kind of funny when he briefed us."

A frown furrowed its way across her brow. "Is that true?" she asked, looking from Angie to Hugh.

Both nodded.

"He wasn't himself," Hugh offered.

"Very distracted," Angie agreed.

Sabrina wished she could tell them about his impending retirement and how that was likely the distraction. "He has a lot on his mind." She thought of the other thing she and Marx had last talked about. "Hugh, did you get that internal surveillance set up in my apartment?"

Big Hugh looked confused. "What surveillance?"

"Marx was…" He'd forgotten she realized. It wasn't like him, but their director had a lot on his mind. "Never mind. We can take care of it when we get back." She couldn't dwell on that right now. This mission had to be her only focus. With that in mind she made up her mind about something else, as well. "I think I'm going to have a talk with Drake."

Angie didn't look convinced that was a good move. "I'd watch my step with him if I were you. I'm thinking he might be a little slippery."

"A lot slippery," Hugh suggested.

Trainer refrained from comment which, in itself, shouted that he totally agreed. Her friends liked Drake, she could tell. They just wanted to be on her side…to be supportive.

"Don't worry," she said, heading for the door, "I've been handling the situation with him for the past thirty-six hours. A few more minutes won't be anything I can't deal with."

She wondered, though, as she left the room, if she was kidding herself. Had she really handled the last day and a half with Drake or had she simply reacted?

Who was to say which of them had actually been in charge? Drake was damned good at manipulating circumstances to come out the way he planned. Maybe she just thought she'd been in control.

She was tired of trying to analyze the situation. She wanted answers.

Now.

She knocked on the door of the room he'd been assigned. He answered promptly, didn't make her wait.

"We need to talk."

"Come in." He opened the door wide for her to enter and then closed the door behind her.

She didn't waste any time. "I want some answers, Drake. I'm not satisfied with this sudden compulsion you have to protect me. And I'm definitely not going along with your accusations against Ledger."

Drake had discarded his jacket. The sweater and jeans looked like they had been tailor made just for him. The fit was perfect. Too perfect to have come off the rack, yet she knew they had.

The IT&PA paramedic who worked with Control, but was brand-new to the team, had checked him out and properly dressed his ribs for support. It would take an X-ray to determine if there were any fractures. Since they didn't have an X-ray machine handy, the injury was treated as if the fractures had been confirmed.

Drake considered her statement for a minute or two. Just long enough to have her on the verge of tapping her foot with impatience.

"I can see how you would feel that way. I wish I could give you more, but I can't. Not yet."

"You mean you won't," she challenged.

"That's right."

At least he admitted it.

"You stand by your initial explanation that your involvement in this operation is about protecting me. And somehow you believe this is about Ledger."

"I believe this is about someone close to you."

"Why can't you just tell me whatever it is?"

That blue gaze settled heavily onto hers. "Because I know you, Sabrina. You'll only believe what your eyes see."

That he would still, after all this time, hold out on her made her furious. "Then I guess we have nothing else to talk about."

He let her walk away.

As she closed the door she hesitated in the hall, somehow unable to just walk away.

She had the overwhelming sensation that things would never be the same after tonight; she just didn't know in what way.

The urge to speak directly to Marx almost sent her in search of Trainer. He wasn't on-site, but Trainer could reach him. No. She didn't want to do or say anything that would add any additional stress for him right now. Marx had enough to worry about. The team had noticed that he wasn't himself. Besides, he would blow a fuse if he knew she'd let Drake in on this mission.

She closed her eyes and fought the wave of uncertainty.

Opening her eyes and moving away from

Drake's door, she reminded herself that she had to keep her wits about her.

For now, she needed to review the profile on her target, as well as the floor plan of his residence. Then maybe she'd rest for a while before making the final preparations.

No mistakes.

She'd promised Marx she'd be extra careful on this mission. No way was she letting him down.

Trusting Drake again was likely mistake enough.

THE ESTATE belonging to Pierre Dubois was built like a fortress, with twelve-foot-high walls.

As much like a keep as it looked on the outside, the interior was palatial. No expense had been spared, from the marble floors to the ornately crafted towering ceilings. Luxurious furnishings and elegant decorating reeked of old money. This man had class, not just money. Even his guests were the cream of the crop.

As usual, Sabrina's gown fit like a glove. Her hair had been arranged in a classic twist, utilizing the comb she would need later in the evening. The shimmering gold stilettos felt amazing on her feet, and looked it, too.

Angie and Hugh looked divine in their royal costumes. Both were born actors. They'd definitely missed their calling.

But the best dressed person was, without question, Eric Drake.

The old-fashioned tux and the Phantom mask lent the perfect air of mystique. He looked amazing. For some reason she felt the need to notice, to pay particular note. Everything about the evening felt *final* somehow.

Between Marx's news about retiring and the visit to her family in Kansas, her emotions were all out of sorts. That had to be what this whole feeling of imminent doom was about.

Focusing on the mission, Sabrina mingled. She floated around the room in her regal gown and flirted with all the men. Drake stayed close behind her, speaking when necessary.

It didn't take Sabrina long to catch Pierre's eye. He followed her progress around the room. He smiled each time she glanced his way. She watched the number of drinks he had as the night progressed, ensuring that she nursed hers. Despite the minute amount of alcohol she consumed, she put on a show that gave the impression she was just a little tipsy.

When a few of the guests had started to dance, she turned to Drake and said, "Dance with me."

When he pulled her into his arms, though she had anticipated the move, her breath hitched. He held her closer, perhaps too close, but she didn't complain. She wanted to feel the strength of his arms and the magnetism of his pull.

"You always were a good dancer," she commented.

"A dancer is only as good as his partner."

Her fingers itched to make a trail up and around his neck, but she had to remember where she was. For her target's benefit, she angled her head so that her face aligned with Drake's. The closeness of their lips would no doubt intrigue the older man who was likely to be as into voyeurism as he was younger women.

The feel of Drake's breath on her lips was almost her undoing.

"You do like playing with fire."

She stared into those searching blue eyes and told him the truth. "Very much so."

"There's something I must tell you now…before it's too late."

Tension whipped through her. "What do you mean, before it's too late?"

"I didn't simply resign from Interpol two years ago. I left under a bit of a dark cloud."

Some part of her had known that nothing he'd told her so far was as simple as he'd wanted to make it seem.

"What kind of dark cloud?"

"I was accused of treason by one of my colleagues, but no grounds were found for the accusation."

Treason? Impossible. Drake might be many things but a traitor he was not.

"Who would accuse you of such a thing?"

"Someone you trust, I fear."

She knew absolutely no one who thought badly of Drake's professional reputation. Her friends didn't care for his way of handling his personal life, but no one could complain about him on a professional level.

"There has to be some mistake. I don't know anyone who considers you less than a legend at Interpol."

"That's where you're wrong, I'm afraid. Marx and Ledger know everything."

How could Marx know? He would have told her…wouldn't he? Marx was like a father to her. He would never hide something this important from her. Unless, of course, he thought he was protecting her. And Ledger would have said something, surely, if for no other reason to help her forget Drake.

"Are you certain about that?" This sounded completely wrong.

"I'm certain."

"Then why didn't Marx mention your status to me before?"

"Some things I can't tell you just yet," Drake said, his tone filled with urgency. "But the one thing you must remember is that your most deadly enemy just now is someone you know and trust."

There he went again. She had no reason to distrust anyone close to her. Sure, Marx was behaving a little off-kilter, but he had good reason. And, yeah, Ledger had crashed back into her life, but the timing wasn't his choice.

She stopped. "I think this dance is over."

"Remember what I said, Sabrina."

She turned her back on him and surveyed the crowd. Time to acquire her target. Time to make Drake suffer a little. Let him wonder what she and the target were up to in his lavish suite of private rooms. The way she'd had to wonder two years ago.

A smile beamed across her lips when her eyes landed on Pierre Dubois. He gave her a little nod, which was all the invitation she needed. She swept across the floor, weaving around couples chatting or dancing until she reached her target.

"I must say, madame, you do look smashing in that exquisite gown." Pierre Dubois kissed her outstretched hand.

Sabrina laughed a deep, throaty sound. "Why thank you, sir. Though I feel inclined to admit that after only one dance it has grown quite cumbersome."

He raked her body with keen gray eyes. "Perhaps you'd feel more comfortable in something less burdensome."

She tiptoed so that she could whisper in his ear. "I've always found less is more."

He kissed her hand once more, his lips lingering there. When his gaze met hers this time, he all but purred, "We could retire to my suite for a brief respite. That is," he qualified, "if your dashing escort won't be opposed."

She looped her arm in his. "That would be divine." She pulled his arm close enough to brush against her breasts. "My escort is not my lord and master."

"Excellent."

Dubois led the way through the crowd, speaking to those who spoke to him first but not bothering to introduce Sabrina. Not that he'd even bothered to ask her name. He wasn't worried about who she was, only what she had to offer beneath her glittering dress.

As they ascended the curving staircase, she caught a glimpse of Drake from the corner of her eye. She wanted him to sweat the next few minutes. She wanted him to wonder if she would go to the same extremes to achieve her goal as he had two years ago.

The upstairs corridor stretched from east to west, providing separate access to each wing of the house. The master suite of rooms was in the west wing.

The double doors opened into an opulent sitting

room. Another set of doors would lead to the sleeping area where the safe was.

She didn't take the time to admire the decor. Instead she turned her back to her host and got straight to the point.

"Can you take care of the zipper?"

"Why, of course."

She felt his hands shake as he lowered the long, narrow zipper, revealing the formfitting red silk teddy beneath. Sabrina allowed the dress to drift down to the floor and then she stepped out of it. The gold stilettos were a perfect accent to the wicked red teddy. Lace and silk, and not much of it, were all that covered the absolute essentials.

Her target gawked.

"I'd love a glass of wine or champagne."

"Oh." Her request seemed to startle him. "Of course."

"Wait." She tugged on the sleeve of his elegant jacket. "Why don't I take care of the drinks while you take care of all these clothes you're wearing?"

He nodded, his eyes widening in anticipation.

She walked over to the bar, making sure each deliberate step was a precisely executed act of seduction.

When she glanced back at her target he seemed to be standing there in a trance. As she watched he abruptly jerked into action, shedding his jacket and tearing at the buttons of his shirt.

She poured the first glass of wine, angling her body where he couldn't see her hands. She dumped the contents of the ring into the second glass before filling it. The meager trace of powder dissolved instantly. No stirring was necessary. Absolutely tasteless, Hugh had assured her, and fast-acting.

Good thing. She had no desire to end up in bed with this pretentious old bastard.

"Here we are." She crossed back to where Dubois waited, twisting her hips dramatically. Hanging on to the glass in her left hand, she offered the one in her right to him.

He took the glass and guzzled the wine as if he'd been dying of thirst or required fortification for what was to come.

His shirt and cummerbund were on the floor next to his jacket, leaving his upper torso clad only in a white T-shirt. She surveyed his trousers.

"Would you like some help with those?"

His nostrils flared. "That would be very nice."

Sabrina sipped her wine, then set both her glass and his aside before slowly settling on her knees in front of him. She heard his harsh intake of breath.

First, she tugged off his right shoe. She tossed it aside and reached for the left. He managed to lift his foot, but he staggered a little with the effort. She couldn't be sure if that was normal for him or if it was the spiked drink.

When her fingers reached for the fly of his trousers, his mouth dropped open and another of those ragged breaths echoed in the otherwise quiet room.

She released the button and slowly lowered the zipper. The play of anticipation on his face made her worry that somehow the powder wasn't sufficient, or maybe she'd given him the wrong glass. But she felt fine, so that couldn't be the case.

Tugging the trousers down the length of his legs she tried not to look at the tent his boxers now formed. He lifted his right foot and she pulled the trousers free. When he lifted the left foot with no trouble, she really started to worry. Why the hell wasn't this working?

She thought of the water Ed Segelman had drank and how the reaction had been delayed. She did not want that to happen in this case.

When Dubois's trousers were tossed aside, she started to rise but he stopped her with a hand on her shoulder. The look in his eyes told her exactly what he wanted.

Oh, damn.

Hoping like hell he wouldn't last more than another ten seconds, she reached for the waistband of his boxers.

To her supreme relief he wilted at the knees first, crumpling into a pile right in front of her.

"'Bout time," she muttered.

She checked his pulse just to make sure she hadn't killed him.

They'd been gone from the party approximately ten minutes. Time to get down to business. First, she closed the double doors that led into the sitting room from the corridor. Then she hustled over to the ones leading into the bedroom. She didn't bother putting her dress back on. She would be able to move more freely without it.

In the bedroom, she turned on the lamp next to the bed and climbed onto the kingsize mattress. The lovely landscape portrait hanging over the bed camouflaged the safe. The picture and its wide gold frame were fasted to the wall with a piano hinge. It opened away from the safe like a door.

She removed her watch and pressed it, back side down, to the safe near the dial and gave the small stem a twist.

One full turn of the safe's dial to the right. The display on her watch remained blank for a moment then it flashed and exhibited the first numbers in the combination. A few turns later and she had the full set of necessary numbers. She slid the watch back onto her wrist and then entered the combination. The door opened with a simple click.

Inside, a number of items were stored but only one contained what she needed.

She reached for the handheld computer and pushed the On button.

Nothing happened.

A frown marred her forehead.

She tried again.

Still nothing.

Not good.

"Trainer."

Then she remembered that her communications was built into the bodice of the dress. So maybe getting undressed in the other room hadn't been such a smart move. Fine, she'd just take the palm-size computer into the other room with her.

"Your part is done here, Agent Fox."

Sabrina stalled next to the bed.

Movement in the dark on the other side of the room had her prepping for fight or flight.

Then recognition slammed into her brain.

"Ledger?"

Colin Ledger stepped from the shadows.

"You may get dressed now."

What the hell was he doing here?

"I need to contact Trainer," she explained. "I can't access the codes."

"There are no codes."

Whoa. Obviously the guy had lost his mind. Maybe all the men in her life just now were a little off. Except Hugh and Trainer, of course.

"My mission was to copy the codes." She had the comb containing a digital camera in her hair to prove it. Ledger had to be wrong.

"Doing it this way wasn't my idea, Fox. I want you to know that up front." He seemed to square his shoulders. "This mission was a setup to draw Drake out into the open. We've got the situation under control now. All you have to do is relax and let us take it from here."

Drake had said that he'd been accused of treason by one of his colleagues. Surely, he hadn't meant Ledger. What the hell was going on here?

"You think Drake did something wrong two years ago?"

"I'm afraid you don't have all the facts, Fox."

"Maybe not, but I will have them before this goes any further." She knew Marx wouldn't go along with this. This whole thing had to have been set up by Ledger and Interpol.

"We received intel that Drake was working with an old enemy. Using his vast knowledge of Interpol as well as IT&PA to benefit his new endeavor. He has to be stopped."

"You really expect me to believe that Drake committed treason? That he betrayed his country? That he's doing that now? Ledger, you can't possibly believe that," Sabrina said.

"It's out of my hands, *Sabrina*."

He moved a step closer to her. She tensed. He noticed.

"You're still in love with *him*, aren't you?"

Why the hell would he ask her that? "No," she lied.

He smiled sadly. "That's why it never worked

between us. I knew you were still in love with him, but I had to try."

"What does that have to do with this mission? With the here and now?"

"We knew that Drake was watching you. Setting up this pseudomission and leaking the rumor that you had been targeted for execution was the only way to lure Drake out. You know how good he is. Finding and stopping him would have been impossible. So we let him believe you were in danger."

Ledger was serious. That was the reason someone had broken into her apartment…had followed her. The epiphany hit her hard. Surely Marx hadn't gone along with all this.

Another realization hit her. "The men on the train were sent by you?"

Ledger nodded. "We thought we could intercept you at that point and save all this trouble, but we should have known Drake would be too crafty for a ploy that simple."

"Who is the *we* you keep talking about? Is this Interpol's way of trapping Drake? Did Interpol use IT&PA resources to clean up their own problems, real or imagined?"

"You don't understand, Sabrina. This is—"

"You know what?" She shook her head. "I don't even want to know."

She wasn't going to be a party to anyone being railroaded. This whole setup didn't sit right. Heilman, the courier, had said their people tried to kill him. They did kill him, she amended, her apprehension suddenly taking off. Four goons tried to kill both her and Drake.

This was not the way IT&PA did business. It wasn't the way Interpol did business. This was out of control.

She stopped, almost at the door, and faced Ledger. He still stood where she'd left him, watching her walk away. He looked tired...and sad. If he was the enemy Drake had warned her to watch out for, why didn't he try to stop her?

This whole thing just kept getting more bizarre.

"You can't believe this is right," she urged. "You have to see that this is all wrong." Ledger wasn't her enemy. He couldn't be a traitor any more than Drake was.

"I'm certain we'll both understand when the time is right," he allowed. "For now, you and I should go. Control is taking Drake into custody as we speak. This will all be over soon."

So that was why Control was on-site.

They were here for Drake.

They would never take him alive.

The realization sent a chill through her.

"I won't let you do this." She lifted her chin, stared defiantly at Ledger. "You're wrong."

She started for the door once more.

She had to warn Drake.

Before it was too late.

CHAPTER FIFTEEN

"I UNDERSTAND you're looking for me."

Sabrina stalled halfway to her destination. Drake stood in the open doorway, his face dark with anger.

Ledger looked as startled as her to find him there, but he recovered quickly. "Drake, good to see you old chap," he said.

Sabrina blinked, felt even more confused.

That was when Ledger drew his weapon.

What the hell was he doing?

"Step aside, Fox," Ledger ordered.

She looked from him to Drake, who was also brandishing his weapon now.

She was the only one without a gun handy. But then, she hadn't expected to need anything other than the contents of the poison ring.

"You were the one who set me up to look like a traitor," Drake accused.

Sabrina felt shock rumble through her. Had Drake been right? Was Ledger the enemy? Not just now, but two years ago, as well? How could that be?

"I did nothing of the sort," Ledger hurled back. "You were the one who crossed the line. The rest of us had to pick up the pieces."

Drake stepped farther into the room, around Sabrina.

She had to stop this, they would kill each other.

"I didn't leak that information two years ago. I was set up," Drake argued. "You were looking for a reason to make me look bad, Ledger. My fall from grace put you a little higher up the food chain. You knew they would look to you next for moving into the position of director at IT&PA. But you didn't do it alone."

Sabrina was afraid to move. She wanted to call for help, she prayed that Trainer could hear what was going on via her dress lying on the floor across the room.

"This is getting us nowhere," Ledger countered. "Why don't we let our superiors sort out the dirty details?"

Sabrina felt air fill her lungs. Thank God. Reason had entered the discussion. Even if it had come from the enemy. But if Ledger was the enemy, why didn't he just shoot both her and Drake?

"What?" Drake demanded as if Ledger's reason fueled his fury. "You're not going to kill me? Wasn't that what you were ordered to do?"

A new wave of shock rumbled through Sabrina. Ledger had been ordered to execute Drake?

"I have no intention of following through with that order, Drake, unless you force my hand."

"Just stop." Sabrina put herself back in the line of fire between the two men. She looked at Ledger. "You were ordered to execute Drake?"

Ledger heaved a sigh. "Yes."

She turned to Drake. "What the hell did you do to make Interpol order your execution?"

He shook his head, disappointment in those blue eyes. "If you have to ask, then there's nothing I can say to convince you of the truth."

Regret pricked her. She hadn't meant the question to come out the way it did.

Where the hell was her team? Control was just downstairs. Why the hell hadn't they come up here? Why hadn't anyone showed up to back her up? Trainer had to be hearing this.

"The order didn't come from Interpol."

Sabrina's gaze jerked back to Ledger. "What're you saying?"

"It wasn't supposed to end this way," a new voice said.

Sabrina did an about-face.

Anderson Marx. Despite the gold mask and long black cape, she would recognize him anywhere.

He held a weapon aimed directly at her.

"Looks as though we have the proverbial standoff, gentlemen," he said to Ledger and Drake as he tore off his mask.

That was when the shocking truth hit Sabrina. It was Marx who wanted Drake dead. But why? "You set up Drake? Made him look like a traitor?"

The words echoed in the tense silence. Why would this man, a man she trusted implicitly, do this? That he hadn't put in the order for Hugh to set up surveillance in her apartment made sense now. It wasn't necessary because Marx knew who'd broken into her apartment and who'd followed her. He was in on all this.

"I did what I had to do." Marx shook his head. "Interpol has no business trying to run my organization. IT&PA was my creation. No one," he said, "has the right to run it but me."

"So you ordered Ledger to kill Drake," she asked, disbelief making her voice wobble. How could he do this? Seeing the wild look in his eyes explained all she really needed to know. The idea of losing control of IT&PA had driven him over the edge.

"Actually," Marx said, his tone as well as his expression suddenly resigned, "Ledger and Drake were supposed to kill each other. I knew Drake wouldn't go down without a fight. I hoped Ledger would go down with him."

That was why he'd urged her to take care on this one, Marx hadn't wanted her caught in the crossfire. That should have made her feel a little better, but it didn't. He wanted Drake and Ledger

dead, putting off the Interpol transition yet again.
Perhaps indefinitely. Calling Drake a traitor last
time had done the trick. Now, Marx wanted to do
the same but he couldn't repeat the same scenario
without drawing suspicion. What better way to
accomplish his goal than by setting up this show-
down. Everyone would assume Drake and Ledger
had killed each other over the past…over the girl
they both wanted. The two had always been
fiercely competitive. And if Ledger had gone on
record in any capacity related to the suspicion of
Drake's treason two years ago, the motivation for
the confrontation was solid. Marx had devised the
perfect plan.

"But I knew better than to assume this would
go down without a hitch," Marx said, drawing
Sabrina from her troubling thoughts. "So I came
personally just to make sure it was finished."

To Sabrina's surprise, Drake lowered his
weapon. What was he doing?

"Your time is up, old man," Drake urged. "You
should have moved on. Getting rid of myself and
Ledger isn't going to stop Interpol from taking
the reins. Put down your weapon and do this
right…by the rules."

"You of all people know that following the
rules is overrated." One corner of Marx's mouth
lifted in a wry smile. The aim of his weapon
shifted toward Drake. "Getting rid of the two of

you would buy me some more time. That's all a man my age can ask for."

Marx had ruined Drake's career. He had been prepared to have Ledger and Drake fight to the death, all so he could stay in power a while longer.

How could she have misjudged him so badly?

She'd admired and respected him...thought of him as family. He was her mentor. When had he crossed this line?

That was when she did maybe the stupidest thing in her life. She stepped in front of her director, blocking the aim of his weapon at its target.

"If you plan to do this," she said resolutely, "then you'll have to kill me first."

Anderson Marx, the man she had cared for deeply, the man who had taught her how to be a spy, looked directly into her eyes and did the last thing she would have believed him capable of.

He pulled the trigger.

The bullet grazed her right arm as she went down, hitting the floor hard with Drake somehow beneath her. His quick thinking was all that had saved her a possible lethal hit.

Another weapon discharged.

She scrambled up just in time to see Marx crumple to the floor.

Ledger looked stunned, the weapon in his hand still aimed at the place where Marx had stood.

Drake was next to Ledger before Sabrina could

think what she should do next. He pushed Ledger's arm down, pointing the muzzle to the floor. "He left you no choice," Drake said quietly as if he understood exactly what Ledger was thinking at that moment.

Ledger nodded. "Bloody hell."

Sabrina couldn't wrap her mind around all that had just happened.

"Let me have a look at that."

She glanced up at Drake who was fussing over her arm. He'd pulled out his handkerchief and was attempting to stop the blood. It was nothing…a flesh wound. She didn't even feel the wound, but then she was in shock. She knew it. From the way Drake looked at her, he obviously knew it, as well.

"He was willing to do anything," she murmured, more to herself than to Drake. His gaze met hers. "Destroy your career, execute all three of us…just to stay in power."

Drake sighed wearily. "It's the spy business, Sabrina. Power is the name of the game. Sometimes it takes over."

He was right. For the first time in all the years she'd been doing this, she realized that it was all about power.

And there was nothing wrong with that. As long as the power was in the right hands.

She looked down at Marx lying dead on the floor. He had betrayed all of them. Most of all, he had betrayed himself. People had started to filter into the room. She heard Angie's voice, then Hugh's. Something about communications having been cut, leaving them all in the dark. Medical personnel filed in next. The four members of Control who'd been downstairs during this whole ordeal poured into the room. Even Trainer left his post and showed up. No one could believe what Marx had done.

None of it really sank in for Sabrina during the next few hours.

Marx had tried to kill her. He was dead. Gone.

She was still alive...but she couldn't feel anything at all.

CHAPTER SIXTEEN

SABRINA SHOOK the snow off her coat before entering the UN Plaza building. She hoped the weather conditions didn't cause any additional delays at the airport.

She hustled through security with her bag of gifts and her one suitcase. It was Christmas Eve, and she had a flight in just three hours. But before she could head to Kansas, she had to drop her gifts by to her friends at work.

Once she'd cleared security, she raced for the elevator in hopes of beating the crowd already lining up behind her at the security checkpoint.

The doors slid open, and she relaxed a bit.

Seconds later, she stepped off the elevator onto her floor. It felt different being here now…knowing what she knew about Marx's betrayal to IT&PA. He'd been buried yesterday. Even knowing what she did, Sabrina would still miss him.

"Good morning, Miss Fox." Heather beamed a smile in her direction. "I thought your vacation started today."

"It does, but I had a few last-minute deliveries." She placed Heather's gift on her desk. "Merry Christmas, Heather."

"Why thank you, Miss Fox!"

It didn't matter how old a person got, everyone loved getting Christmas presents. Sabrina left her suitcase at reception. She could pick it up on her way out.

She found Trainer, Hugh and Angie hanging out in Hugh's office.

"Merry Christmas, guys." She passed out the gifts, including an extra one for Angie's kids.

Angie and Hugh produced gifts for Sabrina. "I'm boycotting Christmas this year," Trainer announced when he didn't do the same.

"Actually," Angie said in an aside, "he forgot. Left them at home. I know for a fact he bought gifts since I had to give him a list of things I thought you'd like."

"Ang, you are not to be trusted," he groused.

"Don't worry about it," Sabrina urged. "We'll all have something to look forward to next week."

Trainer's dark mood didn't lift. "I suppose so."

Sabrina hugged her friends. "Merry Christmas, guys."

Things were going to be different around here, but they still had each other. When they'd finished hugging and discussing their respective holiday plans, Angie walked with Sabrina to the new interim director's office. Colin Ledger. He would be officially named the new director, eventually, when internal affairs had closed their investigation into this whole mess. The investigation was nothing more than a technicality to keep NSA happy. For now they labeled Ledger as interim director.

"I guess things are still over between you and Drake?"

Sabrina smiled patiently for her dear friend. "Things have been over for two years, Angie."

Angie stopped outside the reception area leading to Director Marx's former office. "Look, I know this is none of my business but I'm going to say it anyway."

Sabrina braced herself. This was one subject on which she didn't care for her friends' advice.

"I saw the way he looked at you, Sabrina. The man cares deeply. There's no doubt in my mind. You're the only one who doesn't seem to see it."

So she didn't hurt Angie's feelings, Sabrina hugged her. "I appreciate your saying so, Angie, but that doesn't change how I feel. Drake and I are over."

Angie nodded. "Well, have a great holiday."

When Angie had disappeared down the hall, Sabrina made her way to Geraldine's desk. "Merry Christmas." She placed a small package on the secretary's desk.

"Sabrina, how thoughtful of you!" She jumped to her feet and gave Sabrina a hug.

When she stepped out of the embrace, Sabrina asked, "Is he in?"

Geraldine nodded, a flash of regret in her eyes. "In fact, I was just about to call for you. He wants to see you."

Sabrina thanked her and headed for her new boss's door. When she opened the door to his office, she stalled.

Drake was there.

The realization stunned her, she suddenly wanted to run the other way. But she didn't. There was no reason for her to avoid the past any longer.

"Sabrina, please join us." Ledger stood and gestured for her to take a seat next to Drake. "I wanted you to be the first to know that Drake has been fully exonerated and offered reinstatement, if he desires to return to Interpol." This he said with a glance in Drake's direction. "We need him. As we need you." The appeal in his gaze this time was about her staying on at IT&PA. They both knew there could never be anything romantic between them…even if she had wanted that and she hadn't.

"Actually, I'm late for my flight," Sabrina said. Maybe she wasn't going to let the past haunt her any longer but she couldn't discuss the situation right now.

Drake lunged to his feet. "Sabrina, I—"

"I really have to go. I have a flight and I'll barely make it as it is." She managed a cordial smile for Ledger. "I'll see you next week, sir. You can count on that.

Ledger said something else to her, but she wasn't sure exactly what it was since she rushed out so quickly.

She couldn't get to the elevators fast enough. She almost forgot her suitcase. Emotions burned in her eyes. She couldn't remember the last time she'd cried, she suddenly felt as if she would break down at any second.

Marx was dead. Ledger had taken over his office. That was good…she could learn to live with that. Time would heal the betrayal she felt at what Marx had done.

But time wasn't going to change the other.

"Sabrina."

Oh God.

"I have to go." She didn't look back at Drake. Couldn't.

The elevator doors opened just then, thankfully.

She didn't hesitate; she rushed into the car.

To her dismay Drake followed her.

The doors slid closed, and the car bumped into downward motion.

"I wanted to see you before you left for Kansas."

"We have nothing else to talk about, Drake. You need to get that through your head." He hadn't betrayed his country but he had still betrayed her two years ago.

He moved in on her, trapped her between his body and the wall. "What will it take, Sabrina, to convince you how much I care?"

She closed her eyes and let go a heavy breath. "If you don't know, then I can't tell you."

She opened her eyes and found his searching her face.

Why didn't he just let it go?

The truth was, she couldn't tell him what it would take because she didn't know.

"It was me who called you all those times," he admitted. "Just to hear the sound of your voice. I watched you…wanted you. But I stayed away because it was the only way to protect you. Interpol only let me walk away under the suspicion of treason two years ago because they couldn't prove it beyond a shadow of a doubt. They could never connect me completely to the intelligence allegedly leaked. I suspected Ledger set me up to get me out of his way, but I couldn't prove it. The suspicions were dropped but the one condition of my walking away was that I disappear. It was the hardest thing I've ever done. But the cloud hanging over me would have hung over you, as well, if I hadn't gone. There was nothing

I could do to right that wrong until the opportunity presented itself. Marx contacted me with concerns about Ledger."

And the rest was history, Sabrina knew first hand.

The elevator glided to a stop.

"We need to clear up this other cloud," Drake suggested softly.

She didn't want to hear this. She couldn't handle it right now. "I have to go."

He nodded, something about his expression making him look totally lost. "Have a safe flight."

She ducked around him and rushed through the lobby.

The snow was really falling now. She'd be damned lucky to get a cab. She should have left already. Should be well on her way to the airport.

Incredibly, the first cab she hailed eased up to the curb in front of her. Would miracles never cease?

"La Guardia," she told the driver as she opened the door to get in. She settled the suitcase in the seat next to her. She'd only brought the absolute essentials for staying one or two nights visiting her family. And the items she'd hastily bought at the airport gift shop in Paris before her return flight.

As she started to close the door, she glanced back at the glass front of her office building.

Drake stood on the steps, the snow falling around him, watching her go.

For one second, part of her wanted to jump out of the taxi and rush into his arms.

But the second passed. She closed the door and the cab rolled away from the curb.

She didn't know what she wanted from him.

And neither did he, apparently.

If neither of them knew what they wanted, it couldn't possibly mean much.

CHRISTMAS MORNING, Sabrina watched her niece and nephew rip open their presents. The gifts from Paris had really gone over well. She'd gotten all teary-eyed when Leslie and her husband had exchanged gifts last night. The way they had fussed over getting each other the perfect gift really got to her. It was ridiculous, she knew, but she just hadn't been able to help herself.

The kindness and generousness with which Leslie's husband had treated their mother last night had really done some damage.

Now there was one surefire way to tell when a man really loved a woman. He was good to her mother.

Thoughts of Drake attempted to intrude, but she blocked them. She had somehow managed not to think of him or work for the past twenty-four hours. She intended to keep it that way.

She was officially on vacation. Even if it was only for a couple of days.

Sabrina opened her presents from the kids, and Leslie and was thrilled with the funky sweaters and clunky house shoes.

When all the ravaged paper was stuffed into a trash bag and the kids and Leslie's husband were off trying out their new toys, Leslie and Sabrina sneaked into the kitchen for a hot toddy. Their mother was upstairs taking a much-needed nap. All the excitement had worn her out. Or maybe it was the numerous activities she was involved in with her new friends at the assisted living facility.

"This is great," Sabrina said. The Irish coffee really hit the spot.

"Are you sure nothing's wrong, Sabrina?" Her sister scrutinized her for the third time since they'd stolen away from the others. "You don't seem like yourself."

Well she wasn't herself. She felt ready to crumble at the slightest provocation, and that certainly wasn't her.

"I'm okay. Just a lot of changes at work."

Her sister nodded and sipped her brew. "I thought maybe it was boyfriend troubles."

"I told you I don't have a boyfriend."

Leslie raised one shoulder in a halfhearted shrug. "I guess I didn't believe you."

"This is about me being thirty-two and unmarried, isn't it?"

Leslie looked startled. "No, it's not."

"Yeah, right. I know how you and Mom think."

"No, really," Leslie persisted. "It's not about your age at all. It's about the man who called last night."

Sabrina's gaze locked with her sister's. "What man? What call?"

Leslie glanced at the clock. "He said he'd be here around nine and that I shouldn't mention it to you because it was a surprise."

She was going to kill Eric Drake.

The doorbell rang.

"That must be him," Leslie said.

Trepidation seared through Sabrina's veins. "Don't answer it."

Leslie's husband's booming voice greeting someone at the front door confirmed that it was too late.

"I'm sorry," Leslie offered. "I thought you'd be pleased."

"It's okay." Sabrina stood. "I'll take care of it."

She'd had it with Drake trying to horn back in on her life. When she finished with him this time, he would know better than to ever come near her again.

Leslie's husband left them alone in the living room as soon as he saw the fury on Sabrina's face.

"What do you want, Drake?"

A broad smile spread across those gorgeous lips. "I brought your Christmas present. You were in such a hurry to leave I wasn't able to give it to you."

"Just leave, Drake. Leave and—"

"It's Christmas, Sabrina." He took hold of her hand. "You can't kick me out on Christmas."

Damn. Now he was using the holiday as leverage.

"Where's your coat?"

"I don't know," Sabrina said.

"Here it is." Leslie rushed into the room with Sabrina's coat in tow. "Here you go, sis." She waved at Drake. "I'm Leslie. We talked on the phone."

Sabrina's mouth fell open. Had her sister been eavesdropping?

"Nice to meet you, Leslie."

Sabrina snatched her coat from her starry-eyed sister. "Thank you." Then she turned to Drake. "Let's just get this over with."

He helped her into her coat, then led the way outside. A long black limousine sat in the driveway.

She shot him a dark look. "What's this about, Drake?"

"Come on. You'll see."

The driver jumped out and opened the door.

Once they were settled inside, Drake closed the privacy shield between them and the driver, and then he poured two flutes of champagne.

She didn't know why he was doing this, he was wasting his time. If only she could get that message past her brain. The rest of her was way past ready to surrender. But she would die before she let him see how easy this was going to be. Back in New York, she hadn't been able to name what he needed to do, but somehow, on a totally visceral level, she understood that this was it.

"A toast," he offered as he passed one flute to her.

She told her heart to stop its foolish pounding, but it didn't do any good. She didn't want him to see the pulse at her throat fluttering, as it no doubt was.

"To us and the future."

She started to argue, but he'd already clinked her glass and turned up his own. She drank, as much because she needed the fortification as to the toast.

"I turned down Interpol's offer of reinstatement."

She almost choked on the bubbly. "What?"

He sat their glasses back in the minibar. "I said no. I agreed to serve as an advisor on the occasional mission, but I turned down my old job."

"Why would you do that?" Was he doing this for her? Her pulse skipped. Now that, she had to admit, would be a true sacrifice. She knew this man, understood how much his work meant to him. She also knew how hard two years living under the cloud of treason must have been for him. She wasn't the only one who'd suffered.

For entirely different reasons, of course.

"Because I plan to be too busy," he said, dragging her full attention back to him.

She moistened her lips, told herself to stay calm. "Too busy doing what?" Please, please let him say the right thing to make this moment perfect.

He reached into his coat pocket and withdrew a small velvet box. "Taking care of you." He dropped down on one knee in front of her and took her hand. "Sabrina, would you—"

"Wait!" She couldn't catch her breath. "You can't do this. Dammit, Drake, you just can't do this." This was too much, too fast. But it definitely was the right thing to say. Oh, God! He was going to ask her to marry him!

He looked puzzled at her reaction. "Why not?"

A shrug lifted her shoulders as confusion whirled in her head. She didn't know why. She wanted him…but this was more than she had hoped for. This was really fast. "We have issues." It was true. She still hadn't completely forgiven him for the incident two years ago. Or maybe she had, and her pride simply wouldn't allow her to admit it.

"You're right." He tucked the ring box back into his pocket and settled into the seat next to her once more. "I want you to know that I'm prepared to do whatever it takes to earn your forgiveness. No matter how long it takes."

Oh, God. What did she say to that?

She loved him. She knew she did. And Angie was right—he did care about her. Why else would he be here? Going through all this? Turning down his old job?

Because he wanted to make things right between them.

She tried to think of another good reason to slow the momentum. Then it hit her. "We haven't been together in two years. The chemistry may be dead. We may not even like each other anymore." She knew that wasn't true, but it was a hell of a good stalling tactic. The truth was, she wanted to let go and throw herself into his arms...but old habits were hard to break. She'd been protecting herself against this kind of commitment for two years. She couldn't just jump back in with both feet without looking long and hard first. Even though jumping right in was exactly what she wanted to do.

"I don't think the chemistry is dead," he argued with a grin.

He pushed her coat open and leaned in close. He stared at her lips...licked his own. "Tell me what you want, Sabrina, and I'll make it happen. Anything at all."

Anticipation had her heart floundering uselessly. But she couldn't let him off the hook so easily. Yes, he had apologized. He'd confessed his mistake. But would that be enough? With need roaring through her, it was hard to think past it. Maybe she could enjoy the moment and sort out the rest later.

Was what they had once shared worth a second chance?

Damn straight.

"Talk is cheap, Drake. Why don't you stop talking and start showing me what you've got?"

He leaned in even closer, putting his mouth within easy reach of hers. "How much time do you have, Fox?"

"How much time will you need?"

"How about…forever."

Then he kissed her.

He kissed her so long, so deeply that by the time he came up for air she perched on the edge of her first climax. And then he took her, slowly, thoroughly.

When he'd brought her to the very peak of pleasure for the sixth time, breaking all previous records, he murmured a simple question. "You ready to surrender, Fox?"

She pulled his face up to hers. "Surrender?" She shook her head. "Never." She kissed his lips. "Compromise?" She kissed him again. "Maybe."

And that was where they left it.

The perfect solution.
Compromise.
And they had forever to work it out.

* * * * *

Watch for COLBY REBUILT
by Debra Webb,
coming from Harlequin Intrigue
in November 2007

*Silhouette® Romantic Suspense
keeps getting hotter!
Turn the page for a sneak preview
of Wendy Rosnau's latest* SPY GAMES *title*
SLEEPING WITH DANGER

Available November 2007

*Silhouette® Romantic Suspense—
Sparked by Danger, Fueled by Passion!*

Melita had been expecting a chaste quick kiss of the generic variety. But this kiss with Sully was the kind that sparked a dying flame to life. The kind of kiss you can't plan for. The kind of kiss memories are built on.

The memory of her murdered lover, Nemo, came to her then and she made a starved little noise in the back of her throat. She raised her arms and threaded her fingers through Sully's hair, pulled him closer. Felt his body settle, then melt into her.

In that instant her hunger for him grew, and his for her. She pressed herself to him with more urgency, and he responded in kind.

Melita came out of her kiss-induced memory of Nemo with a start. "Wait a minute." She pushed Sully away from her. "You bastard!"

She spit two nasty words at him in Greek, then wiped his kiss from her lips.

"I thought you deserved some solid proof that I'm still in one piece." He started for the door.

"The clock's ticking, honey. Come on, let's get out of here."

"That's it? You sucker me into kissing you, and that's all you have to say?"

"I'm sorry. How's that?"

He didn't sound sorry in the least. "You're—"

"Getting out of this godforsaken prison cell. Stop whining and let's go."

"Not if I was being shot at sunrise. Go. You deserve whatever you get if you walk out that door."

He turned back. "Freedom is what I'm going to get."

"A second of freedom before the guards in the hall shoot you." She jammed her hands on her hips. "And to think I was worried about you."

"If you're staying behind, it's no skin off my ass."

"Wait! What about our deal?"

"You just said you're not coming. Make up your mind."

"Have you forgotten we need a boat?"

"How could I? You keep harping on it."

"I'm not going without a boat. And those guards out there aren't going to just let you walk out of here. You need me and we need a plan."

"I already have a plan. I'm getting out of here. That's the plan."

"I should have realized that you never intended

to take me with you from the very beginning. You're a liar and a coward."

Of everything she had read, there was nothing in Sully Paxton's file that hinted he was a coward, but it was the one word that seemed to register in that one-track mind of his. The look he nailed her with a second later was pure venom.

He came at her so quickly she didn't have time to get out of his way. "You know I'm not a coward."

"Prove it. Give me until dawn. I need one more night to put everything in place before we leave the island."

"You're asking me to stay in this cell one more night...and trust you?"

"Yes."

He snorted. "Yesterday you knew they were planning to harm me, but instead of doing something about it you went to bed and never gave me a second thought. Suppose tonight you do the same. By tomorrow I might damn well be in my grave."

"Okay, I screwed up. I won't do it again." Melita sucked in a ragged breath. "I can't leave this minute. Dawn, Sully. Wait until dawn." When he looked as if he was about to say no, she pleaded, "Please wait for me."

"You're asking a lot. The door's open now. I would be a fool to hang around here and trust that you'll be back."

"What you can trust is that I want off this island as badly as you do, and you're my only hope."

"I must be crazy."

"Is that a yes?"

"Dammit!" He turned his back on her. Swore twice more.

"You won't be sorry."

He turned around. "I already am. How about we seal this new deal?"

He was staring at her lips. Suddenly Melita knew what he expected. "We already sealed it."

"One more. You enjoyed it. Admit it."

"I enjoyed it because I was kissing someone else."

He laughed. "That's a good one."

"It's true. It might have been your lips, but it wasn't you I was kissing."

"If that's your excuse for wanting to kiss me, then—"

"I was kissing Nemo."

"What's a nemo?"

Melita gave Sully a look that clearly told him that he was trespassing on sacred ground. She was about to enforce it with a warning when a voice in the hall jerked them both to attention.

She bolted away from the wall. "Get back in bed. Hurry. I'll be here before dawn."

She didn't reach the door before he snagged her arm, pulled her up against him and planted a kiss on her lips that took her completely by surprise.

When he released her, he said, "If you're confused about who just kissed you, the name's Sully. I'll be here waiting at dawn. Don't be late."

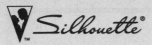

Romantic
SUSPENSE

Sparked by Danger,
Fueled by Passion.

Onyxx agent Sully Paxton's only chance of
survival lies in the hands of his enemy's daughter
Melita Krizova. He doesn't know he's a pawn in the
beautiful island girl's own plan for escape. Can
they survive their ruses and their fiery attraction?

Look for the next installment in the
Spy Games miniseries,

Sleeping with
Danger

by Wendy Rosnau

Available November 2007 wherever you buy books.

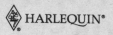

REQUEST YOUR FREE BOOKS!

2 FREE NOVELS PLUS 2 FREE GIFTS!

Silhouette® Romantic

SUSPENSE

Sparked by Danger, Fueled by Passion!

SRS07

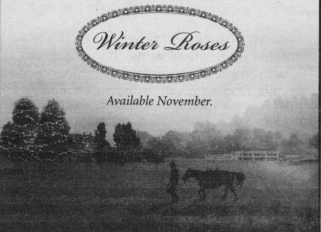